DANGEROUS BOND

MATED TO THE ALIEN UNIVERSE

DETYEN WARRIOR OUTCASTS
BOOK ONE

KATE RUDOLPH

ABOUT THE BOOK

He's as cold as the void of space...

Soulless warrior Drex has been cast out of the Detyen Legion. Eking out an emotionless life on the edge of the galaxy, he knows his days are numbered. There's no future for a man who's already sacrificed everything. Then he rescues Pippa and his whole world is set ablaze.

She can fix any machine, but can she fix him?

Pippa knows all the secrets to the machines that keep Nebula Outpost floating in space, but Drex isn't so easy to figure out. But the more time she spends with him, the more she's eager to know. When tragedy strikes, Pippa and Drex are the only people who can solve the case.

Every clue only leads to more questions, and

even more danger. But Pippa can't walk away from the mystery... or from Drex. He might call himself soulless, but she sees the heat in his eyes. The only question is: will the conflagration burn them to cinders or ignite a bond that lasts a lifetime?

1

PIPPA

"You've gotta be freaking kidding me." I whacked my hammer against the side of the incinerator in the spot guaranteed to get it working again, but all I heard was a sad groaning sound that you never wanted a machine to make.

Okay, not the hammer.

"Come on, baby." I rubbed my hand over the same spot, trying to ignore the indentation from countless engineers applying the same treatment since time immemorial.

Nebula Outpost wasn't the fanciest place in the galaxy, but engineers and techs like me kept it going. And the decades-old incinerators were key to making sure everything ran smoothly.

"How's old G-man doing?" my best friend and

closest co-worker, Noelle Kim, asked, crouching down beside me to study the control panel. Her dark hair was pulled back in a ponytail, and she had a smudge of grease on her chin. If there was only one smudge of grease on my face, I'd call it a good day. That was practically clean.

All the incinerators had names, it beat remembering their serial numbers.

"He's trying to go on holiday." I cycled the power again and bit back a curse as the machine started making even sadder noises than usual. "I think I'm going to be here for a while trying to make this old boy cooperate. Don't wait to take your lunch break."

"Did you piss someone off?" Noelle grinned. "I thought the boss only tortured the troublemakers with ..." She trailed off, searching for words.

"Troublemaking machines?" I suggested. "G-man's usually reliable. Well, as reliable as these old models ever are. I'm thinking it may be a mechanical fault."

"Better you than me." Noelle gave me a pat on the back and stood. "I guess it will just be Darian and me. Your loss."

"You're welcome to him." Darian was a fellow engineer, a big flirt, and an alien, though he'd never told us much about his race. He was a nice guy, but I wasn't looking for love ... or whatever Darian was offering with those sly smiles of his. I had a job to do and was so close to earning my next qualification badge that I could taste it.

"Let me know if you need another pair of hands. I can bring you lunch." Noelle ran her fingers over the hammer indentation and gave me a look.

"I can handle it. Go eat. And bring me a sandwich if you haven't heard from me in two hours." I opened the control panel, and Noelle walked away. My stomach gave a sad little grumble, but I told it to shut up.

There was work to do.

I spent another quarter hour checking every possible connection and diagnostic on my scanner. And, unsurprisingly, nothing seemed to be wrong. Damn it.

I was going to have to go inside the beast.

I looked at the service hatch with a scowl. I hated the thought of going inside the machine. There was always a lingering smell of trash and smoke, and it was hot as hell. Not to mention the nagging fear that the machine would fire up of its own volition and burn me to a crisp.

It was literally impossible. I knew that. Every tech knew that. As long as the door was open, the machine could not fire. But I was only human, and you couldn't ever fully erase a primal fear like that.

"You got this, Pippa Vale. You are a genius engineer who can solve any problem." For some reason, the affirmation didn't make me feel any better.

Screw it.

I slung my gear bag over my shoulder and opened the hatch.

The inside of the machine was bigger than my quarters, but it was just a giant metal tube that stretched up to the top of the level where all the chutes fed their trash. That trash was going to start piling up on the third level if I didn't work quickly.

After a few minutes of inspecting the wiring my panic about getting locked in the incinerator started to fade to the background. It had to if I wanted to get any real work done.

I lost track of time, but after a while I thought I heard footsteps outside. "Noelle, is that you?" I didn't think she'd be back from lunch so soon.

No one answered. Maybe I'd been imagining things.

The thought had barely crossed my mind when I heard a piece of wood clatter to the ground, and the hatch behind me slammed shut, encasing me in metal and darkness.

Immediately, panic surged through me, and I slammed my fists against the door, desperate to escape. The walls felt like they were closing in, and I couldn't suck in a deep enough breath despite the fact that I knew I had more than enough oxygen.

"Help!" I screeched, banging again. G-man was in an older part of the station that was mostly storage and decommissioned parts. No one walked by here, not for fun.

I heard a whisper of sound, and ice froze my veins.

They wouldn't stay cold for long. That was the ignition switch.

Something had powered up the incinerator. And in less than ten minutes, I'd be burned to cinders in flames reaching more than a thousand degrees.

2

DREX

THE OUT-OF-PLACE BANGING of fists on metal diverted me from my scheduled exercise circuit. In three years of living on Nebula Outpost I'd never encountered another person in this sector of the station. It wasn't off-limits, but it was far from anything entertaining.

I paused and tilted my head to listen. The banging was panicked, or, at least, I thought it was. I'd long forgotten what panic—or anything else—felt like.

I wiped a bead of sweat from my brow and considered. I knew where each of my men was supposed to be, so whatever was making the racket could not be one of them. Getting involved in some sort of rescue could bring unwanted attention to myself and the others.

But rescuing people was the right thing to do.

I couldn't feel it, but there were certain principles I had to live by, that all soulless Detyens had to live by, especially the outcasts.

Our species was dying, year by year, person by person. Unmated by unmated. Our planet had been destroyed long ago, the survivors scattered across the galaxies, and all of us living with a terminal diagnosis hanging over our heads: death by the age of thirty if we couldn't find mates.

Except for the soulless.

We were members of the Detyen Legion brave or stupid enough to undergo a procedure to lengthen our lives at the cost of our emotions. The soulless served the Legion until we were used up. And then we were decommissioned ... or we were supposed to be.

Some of us escaped. And now we were here.

I followed the sounds of the banging and found an old incinerator, the door sealed closed and rattling from whatever was inside making a ruckus. The emergency shutoff switch was clearly labeled, and I pressed it and heard the faint hiss as the electricity cut off. I grasped the handle of the door and heaved it open. It was heavy enough that it shouldn't have accidentally fallen closed.

A human woman fell through the opening and down to her hands and knees, chest heaving and tears streaming down her face.

She was unwell.

I crouched down beside her and reached out to help, but she scrambled backward, eyes wild. She heaved in gasping breaths and tried to speak. No words came out.

She was beautiful. It might have struck the non-soulless as odd that I could see that, but beauty was logical. Quantifiable. Her features were symmetrical. Her eyes large and dark, her dark hair falling out of the tie that had held it back. Her body filled out the drab jumpsuit she was wearing, with curves that might have stirred something in me years ago. Now I merely cataloged them dispassionately.

I didn't know what to say. Something had clearly gone wrong. Even without the capacity to fear, I would be uncomfortable if I ended up locked in an incinerator.

"Take a deep breath," I commanded. She flinched, and I lowered my volume. "Deep breath." I demonstrated the motion, sucking air deep into my lungs and letting it out slowly. "Your nervous system must understand it is safe now." Emotion, instinct, and automatic responses were a complex mix that was difficult to navigate once the balance was thrown off, but I'd been soulless for seven years now and had found my equilibrium.

She obeyed, and slowly, her breathing steadied. She wiped at her cheeks, and I saw the smear of ash from the incinerator. Her clothes looked like the sort of thing the maintenance engineers and techs wore, but were rumpled from her ordeal.

She seemed calmer, but I remained still, studying her. There was something ... strange about this woman. She was out of the incinerator and safe. There was no reason for me to remain beside her, no reason to help her regain her breaths. Soulless outcasts survived by remaining in the shadows. We did not mingle with anyone on the station for longer than strictly necessary. Some might have called it a sad life, but we had no other option.

"What is your name?" I asked. I nearly reached out to touch her again, perhaps to help her up, I wasn't sure. But she flinched again, and I withdrew.

Her tongue darted out to wet her quavering lips. "I'm Pippa. The incinerator was malfunctioning, and I ... I ... That shouldn't have happened. How did the door close? Who are you? What are you doing here?

Did you see someone?" Her gaze swung past me, looking for any clue to what was going on.

The avalanche of questions washed over me, but I decided to answer what I could. "My name is Drex. I run down here for exercise. I heard your distress."

She huffed out an ironic sound. "Distress. Right." Pippa pushed herself to her feet and looked around, eyes landing on a small block of wood that had fallen beside the door. "You little bastard." She scooped it up and gripped it hard enough to make her knuckles turn white. "You nearly got me killed." She gave me a bright smile. "Thank you for saving my life. This guy must have slipped. Somehow."

"Of course." I could leave it at that, but I had no reason to keep information to myself. "You should know, the door was locked from the outside, not merely closed."

Her smile slipped, and the little color that had returned drained from her face. "I thought I heard footsteps. But ... no. The autolock must have engaged."

"Perhaps." I didn't have enough knowledge of the mechanism to know.

She blew out a breath. "I have to go fill out about a thousand pieces of paperwork. And someone from engineering might need to confirm all of this. You said your name was Drex, do you have a last name? Clan name? Designation? Anything?"

I hesitated, but only for a moment. "My full name is Drex NaXariz. I live in quarters on level seven."

Pippa grinned, and at that same moment, my stomach felt strange. Possibly a delayed physiological response to the danger. "Maybe I'll see you around, then, Drex."

She reached out and patted my arm, and I could feel the warmth of her skin through the layers of my long-sleeve top.

3
DREX

RYKLIN WAS SITTING in silence when I returned to our quarters. The others were nowhere to be seen. The memory of the human woman, Pippa Vale, rested heavily in my mind. With what I knew of her—name, occupation, approximate age—I could look her up in the station's manifest and learn everything that was publicly available.

I didn't.

I had no reason to.

She wasn't a security threat, and she posed no physical threat. She was merely a woman I encountered and assisted by chance.

"You were scheduled to be back nearly an hour ago," Ryklin said, voice flat. He was the second outcast to arrive on Nebula Outpost, about six months after me. Like me, he'd been scheduled for execution, but someone in his chain of command had ensured his escape.

If the Legion ever found us, we'd be considered deserters and executed on sight. They did not think they could trust independent soulless Detyens. Perhaps they were right. None of us—not me, Ryklin, Thalor, Kyrin, Zyrus, or Jorin—had ever caused harm to anyone on Nebula Outpost, but we imposed severe rules upon ourselves.

Group surveillance. Self reporting. Strict schedules. Each of us had shown signs of weakness at least once and had been condemned by our people. If one of us stumbled, it could cost all of us what little life we had left.

"I heard a woman calling for help," I said. "She somehow became trapped in an incinerator. I was able to free her before she was killed." The report felt ... strange ... coming from my mouth, as if something much more fundamental had happened during my assistance of Pippa Vale.

Ryklin tilted his head and studied me. "You interacted with her?"

"Yes." I had nothing to hide. Though we attempted to remain separate from the rest of the populace, there was no strict rule against rendering aid. "I heard her calling for help during my run."

"Very well. We are due for our shifts in less than an hour. Take your meal before we leave." He gave me the instruction as if I needed to be coached.

I didn't acknowledge it.

The jobs the six of us had taken were all low level: cleaning crew, restaurant dishwasher, station renovation, and interior landscaping. They were the kind of positions that were often overlooked but absolutely vital to the running of a place like Nebula Outpost. And none of them required intense security clearance.

Ryklin and I were groundskeepers. The station had highly cultivated and meticulously cared for green spaces that helped to provide the perfect balance of air for the diverse species living together. The two of us mostly raked mulch and replanted things that grew too big for their surroundings. Everything in the green spaces was consumable, and most of it eventually ended up in the restaurants and cafeterias that kept the residents of Nebula Outpost fed.

The jobs the six of us had did not pay well, but they kept us occupied and provided enough income for two small rooms and sustenance. We didn't need anything else.

As I ate my standard rations and Ryklin stared at me, I wondered if Pippa Vale would seek me out again. The thought gave me pause. I had no reason to think about the woman and no ability to want her to make another move.

I needed to put her out of my mind and move on with my life, such as it was.

But she remained in my thoughts throughout my meal and my shift. The soulless couldn't dream, but if I could, she would have gone with me into sleep.

———

PIPPA

"I swear, Noelle, I'm fine." A part of me regretted making the report of the ... malfunction ... of G-man. It was definitely a malfunction. It had to be. Because if it wasn't ... No, I couldn't contemplate that.

"Maybe you should take the day off," my friend insisted, trying to physically shove me out of the changing room where we were both pulling on our uniforms.

"G-man's officially offline until further notice, and Mr. Rexal took me off of all incinerator maintenance for a week. It's all good. Or do you want me to go back in my quarters and stew myself into a panic attack?" Sleep the night before had not been easy. Every time I closed my eyes, it felt like the walls were closing in around me, and I started to overheat. No one had ever accused Nebula Outpost of being balmy.

I needed to work, needed to do something. Otherwise, I'd start climbing the walls.

I slung my tool pack over my shoulder and gave Noelle a bright smile. "It's going to be fine," I assured her.

"What's going to be fine?" That was Fran, a fellow maintenance tech who's frizzy hair was held back with a colorful bandana. She had a stripe of grease on her shoulder from whatever she'd been working on, and she gave me in inviting smile as she pulled earphones out of her ears. She must not have been listening to the conversation as Noelle and I spoke.

She wasn't the only one butting in. "Yeah, are you alright?" Darian stuck his head in the dressing room, grin broad on his handsome blue face. He worked right alongside us keeping the station functioning, and he was a hopeless flirt, though I hadn't ever heard any of the girls talk about going farther than a bit of harmless fun.

He was a Detyen but didn't often discuss what that meant. Based on the few things he'd let slip over the years, I figured there was tragedy in his past, though I wasn't sure if it was personal or if it had to do with his people.

And he looked a bit like Drex. Similar facial structure. Similar coloring with their turquoise skin and dark eyes. Was Drex Detyen? I hadn't bothered to ask, my mind too preoccupied with the fact that I'd almost died.

Maybe if I could find him again, I would ask. The alien man hadn't been far from my thoughts, and thinking of him had helped me quell the panic that rode me all night. I wanted to thank him again. Properly. Though I wasn't sure there was a proper thanks for pulling me out of an incinerator right before I got burned to a crisp. Maybe chocolates?

"Pippa," Noelle said; she nodded to me but was talking to Fran and Darian. "Apparently not even almost getting fried in a malfunctioning incinerator can slow her down."

"What?" Darian's eyes widened. "What happened? Are you okay?" He stepped fully into the dressing room, as if getting closer to me might make the trauma unhappen.

Fran covered her mouth in shock. "Seriously?"

I held up a hand to ward them off. "It's fine. Really. I didn't die. Stop freaking out." The hand I was holding up started to shake, and I curled it into a fist before either of them could notice. I really was fine.

I had to be.

"Don't you miscreants have work to do?" I plastered a fake smile on my face and shooed them out of the room. Noelle lingered for a second, but she eventually followed Fran and Darian out.

I took three seconds to try and get my heartbeat under control.

Unsurprisingly, it wasn't nearly enough time. But my communicator buzzed with my updated repair assignments, and I didn't have any more time to waste on freaking out.

My boss really was taking it easy on me. I didn't have to climb into any tight quarters or do any of the dirtier work involving station sewage. It was all tightening loose screws and fixing malfunctioning lighting arrays. Things so easy that a child could do them.

I couldn't lose myself in this work, and I kept

thinking about the day before. And about the man who rescued me.

It was better to think about him than contemplate the other thing.

I shuddered.

And then I realized I was on level seven. The same level where Drex said he lived. My shift was nearly over, and I had nothing else to do. Going back to my quarters and staring at the walls until I couldn't help but scream didn't hold much appeal. Noelle would probably be busy, and besides, I didn't want to deal with all of her cloying concern.

I needed to get past this.

Or maybe what I needed was some closure.

Screw it.

I found the nearest directory screen on the hallway wall and searched Drex's name. His lodgings came up and pointed me to the other side of level seven. If the universe was giving me a sign, it was probably telling me to turn around and drop it. Getting from one side of level seven involved walking halfway there then taking the lift up to level five, the stairs down to level six, and then another lift to the opposite side of level seven. Crossing the distance would take fifteen minutes, maybe half an hour.

But I still had nothing better to do.

I just had to thank the guy.

The walk took closer to the half hour end of my estimate, and I ended up in a narrow-walled section of the station where cheap, crowded, and strangely quiet quarters abounded.

I stood outside his door and was suddenly nervous. Was I being presumptuous? Drex hadn't exactly been a talker while I freaked out. Would he appreciate a stranger bothering him?

Well, I'd already come all that way ...

Before I could talk myself out of it, I knocked. And waited. And waited.

The room couldn't be that big. In this part of the ship, it was probably not much bigger than a closet with bunks stacked three or four high.

I knocked one last time and told myself I'd count to thirty and then leave.

At forty-five seconds, someone opened the door. It wasn't Drex. He was another blue alien with a similar neutral expression on his face. "Room inspections are not until next week," he said without inflection.

"I'm not here to inspect anything. I wanted to see Drex. Drex Ny—" Crap, what was his last name? There had only been one Drex on level seven, so I hadn't needed to rely on surnames. Now I was hoping I didn't have the wrong place.

"Drex is not here," the alien said. He stepped back, and the door started to slide closed.

I put my foot in to cover the sensor and keep it open. "But he does live here, right? Is he going to be back soon?"

"His business is his own. Please step back." He stared at me as if he could will me to move, and the guy was intense. And ... empty. There wasn't another word for it. Something was missing there, or maybe a screw was loose.

Or maybe I was still a bit rattled and projecting onto strangers.

The guy wasn't going to budge. And he was so much bigger than me it wasn't like I could force him, not that I'd try. "Tell Drex that Pippa came by, will you?"

The man was a statue. "Please remove your foot."

I did. My shoulders slumped as I turned away. I had nowhere else to go, nothing else to do except head back to my room and wallow. Maybe I could delay the inevitable by hitting up the canteen for dinner, but that wouldn't even buy me an hour.

"Pippa?"

My head snapped up, and I grinned when I spotted Drex walking down the hallway. "Hi!" Okay, down girl. That came out way too eager.

"What are you doing here?" Drex asked. "There have not been any maintenance complaints." His expression was neutral and his tone flat. He sounded a lot like the guy who answered the door. I wondered if it was an accent, some quirk of whatever translator he was using.

"I was nearby," I said, which was sort of true in a way that wasn't true at all. "I just finished up my shift, and I remembered you lived on this level, so I thought I'd come say hi."

"Oh." He paused and then inclined his head. "Hello." There was another long pause. "Are you ... well ... after yesterday?"

"As well as can be expected. I have to work or I'd go crazy." I shrugged and tucked my hands in the pockets of my jumpsuit.

"That sounds reasonable."

"Thank you!" It came out a bit stronger than I meant. "My friend Noelle thought I was out of it, but why would I want to stay cooped up in my room all day so I could imagine the walls closing in?" I shuddered.

"You were stuck in an incinerator, not a crusher," he pointed out, still dispassionate.

"Thanks for the reminder." But it made me laugh. "Fears aren't exactly rational, you know?"

He was silent.

"I thought I could buy you dinner, you know, as a thank you." I smiled hopefully, my heart fluttering. I wasn't asking the guy on a date or anything, but it felt a little like that.

"Meals are provided free of charge to all station residents," he said.

"It's just a saying. I wanted to have dinner with you to thank you, got it? What do you say?"

He looked past me to the door to his room. He was silent for so long that I was sure he'd say no. But he finally nodded. "Yes, I'll have dinner with you."

4
DREX

I KNEW I shouldn't accompany Pippa Vale to dinner. The food in my quarters was more than sufficient, and there was no need to walk across the station to access it. I had worked a long shift and would need to sleep soon to maintain optimal restfulness. But there was a look in the human's eyes that made me hesitate.

Hope.

I couldn't feel it. No regrets could haunt me if I walked away. But a sliver of me remembered what it felt like to have hopes dashed on the rocks of reality, and I found myself walking silently beside her as she spoke of her favorite canteen up on level three.

"Ugh, just tell me to shut up if I'm talking too

much." She smiled up at me and rolled her eyes at herself. "I can kind of babble."

"Your voice is pleasant. It is no hardship to listen." The silence in my own quarters could be mind-numbing. Ryklin, Thalor, and I only spoke when necessary. There was no point in chatting. We reported our mental states to one another, gave pertinent information about our work, and left it at that. I spent nearly every non-working hour near Ryklin, and he was still mostly a stranger after more than two years.

"I'll take pleasant." Pippa's pale cheeks were covered in a blush. It wasn't cold, so I wasn't sure what could have caused that. "Your voice isn't so bad, either. You know, when you say stuff." She gave me a long look.

She expected me to speak now.

I could still remember the push and pull of person-to-person interaction. Being soulless hadn't wiped away my memories, it merely put a film over what I knew I should feel and what I actually could.

"You're an engineer?" I prompted. People liked to speak about themselves. It was easy enough to keep that conversation going.

"Yeah, I guess. It is what it is, you know. Machines have a way of speaking to me. I guess I just understand all that cold circuitry and hard logic. Well," she laughed to herself, "that's what the machines *want* you to think."

"What?" Her words didn't make sense. I found myself stepping a little closer as the hallway narrowed and caught a whiff of her scent—it was mostly engine oil and grease, but there was something florally feminine underneath. It tickled something deep in my brain, and I breathed deeper.

"There are repair manuals, right?" She looked at me expectantly, and I nodded. "And they'll tell you to do X, Y, or Z to make the machine work properly. Plug this cord into that outlet, make sure you power it up in this order, whatever. It makes sense. It's how they're designed to function. And ninety, okay maybe seventy-five, percent of the time that works. But then you have to learn the machines' personalities. Some don't like to turn on when they're in the top quartile of their operating temperature. Some need to be knocked in just the right spot to jump-start. And some will do exactly what they're supposed to do, but only if someone comes by every week to tell them just how good of a trash compactor they are. That's Sindy, and she's the compactor on level thirteen," she said the last with a fond smile.

"They have names?" My questions kept coming, but this was relevant to my life. Understanding how the machines functioned could have an impact on my men's survival on this ship.

But the names shouldn't matter.

"All of them have names." Her expression turned serious. "You met G-man yesterday. We have to figure out what happened because we can't have an incinerator eating people. He's usually reliable. Old, but still kicking. Another machine that likes a bit of praise. He's never ..." She shuddered. "But, yes, Sindy is there too. Usually, the name comes from their serial or model number. There's also a food storage unit we call Jacob because the way the bolts are set up looks suspiciously similar to one of our—You know, that's probably more funny if you have actually seen Jacob."

"Certainly."

She gave me a look that I couldn't decipher. "You're ... Never mind."

I didn't understand what she was trying to say. If I were viewing this conversation as a third party, as if this were a military campaign that I had to win, I could do it. But standing here, participating, it was as if my translator was malfunctioning. And yet, I found that I couldn't walk away. "Complete your sentence."

"Bossy much?" She laughed as she said it. "I was just thinking that you're not what I expected."

"What did you expect?" I had not had a conversation that lasted this long since before I lost my soul. Orders were given. Orders were received. Reports were made. There was no need for back-and-forth.

But now my mind felt more engaged than it had in years.

Strange.

"I don't know. It's not bad, I promise. I think I just ... I don't know," she repeated. "You were like this huge knight riding to my rescue. I might have expected a bit of shining armor." She paused in front of the door to the canteen and waited for it to open. "What's your story, anyway?"

We placed our orders, and while we waited for our food, I took a moment to think through my answer. The biggest danger to me and my men was discovery, but there was little chance Pippa had any contacts to the Detyen Legion, or any other Detyens. We were spread far and wide across the universe, our numbers dwindling day by day as the Denya Price claimed more and more victims. With the destruction of our planet a hundred years ago, there was little hope of eventual recovery, not when mates were so rare.

I couldn't think of a lie. For some reason, I had no inclination to, even if keeping my situation a secret was paramount to my safety.

"I was a soldier, once," I said, dancing around the truth as much as I could. "Once that was over, I moved here. Now I'm a groundskeeper." There. The truth, or as much of it as I could provide.

We took our food trays and found seats. I'd chosen a simple protein dish with rice while Pippa's plate was piled high with colorful vegetables and a wobbling dessert that looked like it might collapse if anyone stared at it for too long.

"That's a short story," she said. "Were you a mercenary or something? Fighting pirates? Rescuing maidens? I already know you do that." She waggled her eyebrows.

That tickle in my mind was back, and a part of me wanted to chase it and uncover what, exactly, it meant. Instead, I ruthlessly ignored it. "I was the normal kind of soldier in a normal kind of army. Lots of rules. Lots of structure. What about you?" I needed to stop talking, and the best way to do that was to take control of the conversation. I already knew Pippa loved to talk.

It was no hardship to listen.

"I told you my story. I'm trying to be considerate and not just blabber my way through this entire conversation." She saw someone behind me and waved. "Hi, Darian."

There was a threat at my back. Instinct was supposed to be deadened along with all other emotion, but I could feel the heat, and the hair on the back of my neck stood up. I turned to keep the threat in my sight.

The Detyen threat.

I didn't know him; I'd never seen him before. And judging by the smile on his face, he wasn't a soulless soldier left to rot.

"New friend, Pip?" Darian spared me a look and smiled at her.

That was ... not good. The tickle in my mind grew to static, and my vision narrowed, even as my temples throbbed in pain. I refused to show it. This man could not see any weakness from me.

Pippa's voice was bright as she spoke. "This is Drex. He's the guy who saved me yesterday. Drex, this is my friend Darian. We work together in the engineering department." Her expression faltered for a moment, and I wondered if something looked strange on my face. But she recovered.

"Is there room for company?" Darian asked, setting his tray down at the empty seat.

She winced. "It's kind of a thank you dinner, Dare. Lunch tomorrow?"

Darian laughed it off and scooped his tray back up. "Sounds good. Don't get into trouble!" Then he was gone.

"Are you Detyen like Darian?" she asked. She didn't spare him a second glance, but I kept him in the corner of my eye until he turned a corner and was gone.

"I'm not like Darian." It was the wrong answer to give, too loaded, too ... emotional, as if that was possible. I had to recover. "Yes, I'm Detyen."

"That's cool." She pointed to herself. "Human, if it wasn't obvious. But born and raised on Nebula Outpost. My parents were miners down on the planet before the facilities were shut down. They were killed in that final explosion."

"I'm sorry to hear that."

She took a deep breath and squeezed her eyes shut before smiling again. "Let's not dwell on sad stuff. How's the food?"

There was no more excitement at dinner, and we

both ate quickly, a habit formed from long shifts and short breaks. Pippa escorted me back to the lift down to level seven, still chattering the whole time.

"You know, I wouldn't say no to another meal. Or something," she said, back to the wall while we waited for the lift. "I'm on level three if you ever want to look me up." She leaned forward and kissed my cheek. "Goodnight, Drex."

The lift arrived, and I stepped in. And as the door slid shut, pain exploded behind my eyes. I had to squeeze them shut and clutch my temple, choking back a sound of anguish as if I'd been stabbed through the temple.

I breathed slowly, methodically, using the same training that had helped me survive blaster shots and continue fighting until the battle was done.

By the time I made it back to level seven, the pain had become little more than a dull throb, and I was only a little shaky. In the hallway, I took a moment to collect myself. If Ryklin or the others saw me like this, they'd think I was ill.

Or spiraling.

Just because the six of us had escaped our fates once didn't mean that we were safe. Soulless soldiers did need to be put down at times. Some malfunctions couldn't be cured.

But my mind felt sharper than ever. My senses were honed, the corridor was in higher contrast, though the colors were as dull as ever. The whispering roar of the air filtration system scraped against my blue skin and raised goosebumps. It was like waking up after a century's long coma, though I hadn't realized that I'd been sleeping.

I was still scraped raw when I entered my quarters to find Ryklin and Thalor sitting in silence. They both stared at me as I closed the door behind me and engaged the lock.

"You deviated from you pattern again," Ryklin noted. Thalor was a statue behind him.

"Yes." For a moment I almost explained Pippa, as if she could be explained. But they wouldn't understand. I barely understood it. The static in my mind was fading, but there was still the hint of that tickle, that feeling that something had changed.

"Why did you deviate this time?" he pressed.

"The human I rescued yesterday invited me to dinner. I had no reason to refuse." It was a partial lie.

"We do not engage more than necessary with the other residents of this station. Are you fracturing?" His tone was just as even as always, but there was a glimmer of intensity in his eyes. Normal Detyens, those who retained their souls, had eyes that turned red when emotion rode them hard.

The soulless lost that, along with so much else.

"I am stable," I assured him.

"You should not see that woman again," he warned.

He might have had a point. But I kept my mouth shut. If the chance to see Pippa again came, I would take it. I didn't know why, but I couldn't resist.

5
PIPPA

"Where's Fran?" The changing room was quieter than normal; even Noelle was strangely subdued. I, on the other hand, felt like I was floating on clouds. And, since we were in a space station, maybe we technically were. Drex was not what I expected in a date, and he was quiet. Maybe too quiet. But walking with him, talking, eating, all of that had felt so comfortable, like I'd been waiting forever for the guy to show up.

Ugh! I did not have time for a crush on a stoic alien. Too bad my brain had already made her decision.

"I haven't seen her," Noelle said on a yawn. "Someone got into a fight in the hallway last night, and it woke me. I couldn't get back to sleep." She rubbed her eyes.

"Weird, I didn't hear anything." I was only a few doors down from Noelle, and the soundproofing on my quarters was no better than hers.

"Lucky." She took a swig of her coffee, quickly followed by a second gulp. "Once this kicks in I'll be fine."

I checked my duty roster, and my eyes bugged out. G-man was right there, the third stop on my schedule. But upon closer look, all I had to do was make sure that it was disabled. It wouldn't take more than a minute to confirm all the connections were severed.

I didn't mention it to Noelle. She'd worry and insist on taking the job from me. I didn't want that; I needed to face this thing and get over it. Once I could remind myself that G-man was just a machine, same as any other, and that it wasn't a demonic entity determined to swallow me whole, I'd be fine.

Hopefully.

Two hours later, with my anxiety having plenty of time to churn into bloodcurdling fear, I approached the machine. But before I got close, I noticed strange scuffs on the ground. I crouched down and took a picture, noting it in the file for maintenance to come and clean up.

Okay. That was enough putting it off.

G-man loomed at the end of the hallway, and I approached him like he was a wild tiger with a taste for human blood, my steps slow and overly cautious. Not that there was any outrunning a hungry tiger. The screen was dark and didn't respond to my touch. But there were more of those scuff marks right by the door, and I worried that kids might have been playing near the machine.

The door was supposed to be magnetically locked and impossible to open with anything less than robotic strength. And if anyone successfully opened it without disengaging the lock, the frame would bend.

From the outside, everything looked fine.

I hesitated in front of the door, the memory of being trapped inside still too fresh in my mind. But I had to check.

I put my hand on the handle and tugged.

The door swung open, and something fell out, crashing to the ground and shattering into dust and crumbled pieces.

I screamed and stumbled backwards before the

strength went out of me and I crumpled to my knees and my vision went black.

A deep rumbly voice was the first thing I heard as I came to, a voice I recognized.

Drex.

I opened my eyes, and there he was, crouched over me and brows drawn together. His eyes looked somehow deeper than the normal black I'd dreamt about all night, as if they were tinged with some other color I hadn't noticed before.

"You aren't injured," he said as I struggled to sit up.

I looked down at my uniform and saw the gray dust that had puffed out of G-man. "Someone was in there." *Just like me.* I couldn't say the last part out loud, but he must have realized what I was feeling.

"I contacted the authorities," he said. "Station security is coming to investigate."

"Oh, god." That made me want to crumple up even more. I curled in on myself for a moment before struggling to stand. If station security was coming, I wanted to face them on my feet. "No one was supposed to be in there. This machine was turned off. Do you think some kid ..." I couldn't even finish the thought as the horror of it washed over me.

"Someone had to reconnect the power," he said

cooly. "They would need to know the override codes."

My mind was too hazy and scrambled to make sense of that. "What are you suggesting?"

Before he could answer, three men in the dark red uniforms of station security showed up. They interrogated Drex and I for what felt like hours, but none of them seemed particularly concerned about the fragments of a person that were starting to clump together and float up towards the air scrubbers.

"Looks like it could have been a table," the head security officer speculated as he crouched and studied a long fragment of debris that I was sure had once been a femur. "Maybe someone didn't want to pay the destruction fees and snuck down to use this guy."

The other two guards shrugged in agreement.

"We'll test all of this." He bagged up the debris, and it crumbled to nothing. "We'll try to test all of this. The lab's a bit backed up with that outbreak of food poisoning last month, but we'll figure something out. I'll be in touch if we need more. Move along now, both of you."

I wanted to argue. That was no table. Wood burned to nothing but ash in those incinerators, and

I'd seen plenty of the aftermath of furniture destruction. I opened my mouth to state my case, but Drex put a hand on my back and led me away.

"We shouldn't make trouble," he murmured. "Not if we don't want trouble."

I wished he was wrong, but station security was there to keep order. If they had to take care of solving crimes, it was usually petty theft or assault. People didn't get shoved into incinerators on Nebula Outpost.

We were only a few yards away when I saw something glinting on the ground, wedged between the wall and the floor. I crouched down and plucked it out with my nails.

It was a small necklace with a tarnished silver chain and a blue stone embedded with the swirl of a golden galaxy. The clasp was broken.

I looked over my shoulder to where the security officers were lounging, as if they were on a break rather than investigating something heinous.

I'd seen that necklace before. It belonged to my co-worker Fran. And she hadn't showed up for work today.

She didn't live far from Noelle or I.

I let instinct take me, charging towards the lift with Drex hot on my heels. "Where are we going?"

he asked. My chest was heaving, but he spoke as if we were on a pleasant walk rather than a half-sprint.

"I think I know who was in the incinerator." I gasped the words out and didn't speak anymore. I feared if I tried, I might scream.

We made it up to the third level, and I passed by my door without a second look. There was carpet on the floor up here, so no scuff marks. But Noelle had heard an argument. Had someone dragged Fran out of her room and taken her to the incinerator?

My stomach roiled with the need to throw up. How could they?

Maybe it was an accident. Maybe ...

There was no good solution that ended with a person in an incinerator. We had specific devices to deal with people who died on the station. There would never be a reason for a body to end up in the same place we threw our garbage.

I stopped in front of Fran's door and pounded with all my strength.

No one answered.

I pounded again.

Still nothing.

I put my hand on the door to try and open it, but

Drex placed his own hand on my shoulder. "Step back, Pippa. Don't."

I whipped around. "Why?"

"Station security is supposed to handle this," he pointed out.

"Yeah, because they looked like a real crack team. They probably swept the rest of her into the cleaning chute." That was what finally broke me, and a sob ripped out of my chest as I collapsed forward, against Drex.

He wrapped his arms around me and held me as I cried.

6

DREX

"Something is wrong on the station," I told Ryklin once I returned to my quarters. My skin could still feel the imprint of Pippa's body pressed against me, and the wetness of her tears made the noise in my head roar to something that nearly drowned out everything else. "Station security is incompetent."

"Yes," Ryklin agreed. "That's one of the reasons we've remained safe all this time."

He had a point. I'd seen the corruption of this place up close in my first days here when I found a station security officer cooking drugs in an out-of-the-way storage room.

Any other place would have asked questions of newcomers with insufficient paperwork. But Nebula Outpost was at the far end of nowhere and needed bodies to keep the place running. Ever since the mines on the planet of Nebula had shut down, the place was bleeding people. There was no logical reason to keep the space station operational, but as far as I knew, there had been no talk of shutting it down in the ten years since the final mine closure.

"I have reason to believe that a woman was trapped in an incinerator and killed last night. I saw the remains." Pippa had tried for several minutes, pounding on Fran's door, but no one had ever answered. A necklace and an unanswered knock were far from definitive proof of foul play, but they were the start of something.

"Is that the woman you assisted?" he asked.

"*No*." It came out stronger than anything ever did, and Ryklin gave me a long look. I ignored it. "I was on my standard running path and again saw Ms. Vale examining the incinerator. She opened the door, and the remains fell out."

"Fell out?"

"As if someone perished while pressed against the door." I could speculate as to why. I didn't need emotion to know someone would do whatever they could to get out of an incinerator before it lit up. "I called station security, and they suggested the remains were a table."

Ryklin blinked twice and stared. "Your patterns have changed in the last few days, but I refuse to believe you've started joking."

"Of course not. Pip—Ms. Vale seemed ready to make things difficult. I steered her away, and she discovered a piece of jewelry. She didn't say it in so many words, but I believe someone put this Fran woman into the incinerator on purpose while she was still alive. I think there's a killer on the station." I hadn't suggested it to Pippa, not while she was so fragile. She didn't need to worry any more than she already was.

"That is unfortunate."

"I am going to investigate this." I'd made the decision while Pippa cried. If station security couldn't be counted on, then someone had to do it. I still had all my training from the Legion. And though there was nothing about solving murders, there was plenty about studying people.

"Why?" Ryklin's stare was level and his tone even, but his question carried weight. "There is no need for you to involve yourself."

"I have no desire to be murdered." But that wasn't it. Not completely.

Ryklin was not convinced. "There are thousands

of people on the station. Your odds of survival are satisfactory."

"I do not need to justify my actions to you." Ryklin did not outrank me. Though each of us six outcasts monitored one another, we made our own decisions and lived our own lives, such as they were. "But I would appreciate your help."

"Why?" Ryklin leaned forward, just a centimeter, but it was enough to scream that I had his attention.

"You are intelligent, and we have the same schedule, so work will not be an issue. And if this grows beyond one murder, speculation could fall on us. People look for those who don't fit in. We could very easily become targets of a mob even if security never suspects a thing." It had happened to Detyens before. There had been riots in The Consortium that ended with hundreds of Detyens dead or exiled. News had trickled to the Legion, and we'd collected a few survivors.

"Do you have any suspects?" he asked.

"Not yet. But I'm going back to the scene of the crime." I couldn't investigate while Pippa was crying in my arms. She'd been my priority then. But now she was safely ensconced in her room, and I could get to work.

"I'll join you."

There was no time to waste. We had work in a few hours, but if we left the investigation to tomorrow, I had no doubt that the evidence would be gone. If it wasn't already.

By the time we arrived at the incinerator, station security had left. There was still the dust on the floor, but there was nothing to indicate that this was a scene of a crime and shouldn't be disturbed.

"Tell me again what happened," said Ryklin.

I did as best I could, starting from the edge of the hall where I'd first spotted Pippa and leading up to the moment we walked away.

Ryklin crouched down to study the scuff marks on the floor. "They're irregular."

"Yes, they begin farther down the hallway. Shoes, perhaps." I couldn't say they had come from a struggle, more like someone had dragged their foot.

"Perhaps," he agreed.

"This machine was supposed to be shut down after Pippa was locked in the other day," I said as I approached the controls. "It was assumed to be a malfunction, though I suspect it could have been the same person that did this."

"Or it could have been the malfunction that gave the assailant the idea," Ryklin suggested.

"True." I examined the control panel, but it was

dark and didn't respond when I touched it. All of the wires had been pulled out of the socket, and there was an identity scanner next to the wiring, possibly to log if anyone tried to turn it back on. "I don't think this was here earlier."

"Maintenance might have added it to prevent further tragedy."

"I suppose." The door was slightly open. I wedged my fingers into the opening and pulled until there was a space large enough for me to slide through. "Cover me," I told Ryklin.

"Yes."

The inside of the incinerator was pitch-black until I pulled out my communicator and used the holoplayer feature to project a ball of light that illuminated the cylinder around me. I placed the communicator on the ground at the center of the incinerator to keep my hands free.

Even with the light, there wasn't much to see. The walls were darker towards the bottom, most likely from the daily firings. The grate around the center of the cylinder had been removed, and a square section of flooring was gone as well. Possibly taken by security, though I had no way of knowing.

There was a thick layer of ash covering the bottom of the incinerator, but beneath that I found something metallic that glinted in the light. I knelt down and brushed it off with my hands to reveal a strange metal rod with holes for several pins. I sifted through more of the ashes and found one pin, but no more.

It could have been anything. The incinerators were meant for organic material, but no one was perfect. Surely metal and other goods that couldn't be destroyed by fire ended up in them from time to time.

I brought the metal out with me and showed it to Ryklin. "Any ideas?"

He took it and studied it. "I will do some research. Did you find anything else inside?"

"No." If this truly was a murder, the weapon was too destructive to leave much evidence. "I don't think there's much more to learn here."

"I agree."

We headed back to our room, and I was unsure if either of us could crack this case.

7

PIPPA

I woke up with a scream and tried to bite it back before anyone heard through my room's thin walls. I sat up in my bed and heaved in breaths that racked my whole body. The nightmare tried to cling to me, tried to suck me back into the incinerator and set the fire roaring until I was nothing more than clumps of ash.

Bile rose in my throat, and I clutched my hand to my mouth, breathing through my nose.

You're safe, I told myself.

Yeah, my brain didn't exactly agree with that. But the bile subsided, and I lowered my hand, pretty sure I wasn't going to barf.

The clock on my bedside table told me it was too early to be up. I had a scheduled day off, and even if I hadn't, I was pretty sure my boss would have forbidden me from coming in. I'd forbid it too if I was in the same place. First, I got locked in the incinerator, and then I found the remains of a person. Who knew what trouble I'd bring down next time. Maybe I'd blow up part of the station.

I shuddered. Was I cursed?

I lay back down and tried to close my eyes. All that did was make it worse. I couldn't banish the image of the inside of the incinerator. That had almost been me. I would've been the dust and ash if not for Drex.

Drex. His name was a balm. His arms around me had been all that kept me upright while I pounded on Fran's door until my fist went numb.

I wished he was here with me right now. I could curl up next to him and let him keep me safe from any of the threats that lurked outside in the station.

I wasn't the kind of woman that was looking for a man to protect her. But there was something about Drex that made me feel safe. It wasn't just the way he saved me a few days ago. It was his presence, his strength. If he were here, I might not be so afraid of sleeping again.

When he looked at me, it was like he could peer deep into my soul. Normally, that would freak me out. I mean, I wasn't some super weirdo or whatever, but that didn't mean I wanted strangers looking deep into the depths of me.

But Drex didn't feel like a stranger. It was ridiculous. I'd known the guy for two days, maybe two and a half now. I'd spent just a couple of hours in his company, and I'd done most of the talking. But he felt like someone who had always been there and always would be, like he slotted right into a place I hadn't known had been missing a part.

Okay, the nightmare was making me crazy. If I didn't yank back control of myself, I'd be writing poems for the guy, and I didn't think he'd appreciate that.

Drex, oh Drex,
When I think of you,
I think of sex.

"Oh my god." I smothered my face in the pillow and groaned as I was assaulted by terrible stanzas.

He's tall and mysterious,
and they call him Drex.
He makes this girl yearn for sex.

"What kind of name is Drex, anyway? Rhyme with something else, you asshole." But I was laughing at myself, and that was better than crying in fear.

It was still too early to wake up, but I wasn't going to go back to sleep. I was a little scared to think what would happen if I tried, and my brain decided to scramble together the sexy thoughts and the terror of the incinerator.

Damn it. Mirth gone.

I got out of bed and made the strongest caffeinated beverage that my food processor could handle and stood in front of it, yawning, as I waited for the goodness to be prepared. A minute later, I had a sweet and steamy cup of something, and I clutched it in my hands and sipped gently. It burned my tongue a little, but the pain only made me feel more awake.

Good. I needed to be awake now.

I was tempted to throw on clothes and head down to G-man and take a look around. I didn't trust station security to do a damn thing, not after their joke of an interview and investigation. Fran's necklace was sitting on the small counter beside my food processor, the stone glinting under the kitchen light, accusing me of failing her.

What did that stone know?

I hadn't failed Fran. I barely knew the woman. We'd worked on a few projects together, sure, but were nothing more than polite colleagues and neighbors.

I wasn't going down to G-man in the middle of the night. The halls would all be dim, darkened by the station to simulate a daily schedule. And if Fran really was killed, I didn't want to be wandering the halls in the small hours when her killer might be out there.

I gripped my drink tighter and curled into myself. No, I definitely didn't want that.

But what could I do?

Noelle would probably tell me to hand Fran's necklace over to station security and let them handle that. But Noelle wasn't from Nebula Outpost. She'd come here on a training contract from someplace called The Consortium and stuck around once her education was done, saying she liked the ambiance of the place. Maybe things were different in The Consortium, but here station security existed to make sure shipments happened on time and to keep drunken brawls from turning into riots.

They didn't solve murders.

Murders didn't happen here. At least, not that I'd ever heard of.

Nebula Outpost was a safe place. Yeah, people

got into fights. Sometimes people stole. But that happened anywhere. Murder, though? Not a chance.

Or was that me being naive? What if murders did happen here but they were covered up and never solved?

"Damn it!" My mind was racing, wondering what other secrets Nebula Outpost had been hiding my entire life. I took another sip of my drink and closed my eyes, trying to calm myself down.

I couldn't go down there, not yet. But examining G-man wasn't the only avenue of investigation.

I pulled my entertainment tablet out of the drawer I'd shoved it in when I gave up on a particularly frustrating game and pulled up the duty roster from work for the last week. I knew I was supposed to check on G-man yesterday, but what about the day before that? Maybe I could ask them if anything was amiss. They should have stated it in their daily report, but not everything got filed to the central database in a timely manner.

The duty rosters were always listed in the same format, but for some reason, when I looked at the most recent ones, nothing was there.

"Huh?" I scrolled through the page, wondering if I was missing something. I could find rosters from two weeks ago, but nothing after that.

Was this station security's doing? They'd ask for the rosters too, but I had no idea why they'd pull them down from the online work site. Unless they were trying to stop nosy people like me from researching the problem themselves.

I pulled out my communicator and looked at my photos. I always took a picture of the roster just in case there were any hiccups. And there was G-man's schedule. My photo only went back to two days ago when I got locked in. Then, Darian was in charge of powering it down. Then me again, just to observe that it was, indeed, powered down.

Darian was a hard worker, and he had a way with machines. He wouldn't make a mistake in powering the thing down. But now I had a place to start. He'd tell me if anything was up.

Did Fran have any family on the station? That would be another avenue to pursue. So many of us had lost everyone to the mining disaster ten years ago that there was no guarantee. Both of my parents had been down on Nebula and hadn't made it out. There might not be any next of kin to report Fran's disappearance to. Or to find out anything that might explain why someone would kill her.

Was it really a murder?

I didn't want it to be. But I couldn't believe this

was a tragic accident, not after the same thing almost happened to me and no one was supposed to be near that machine.

Darian would give me answers. I just had to wait a few more hours until he was actually awake to ask.

8

DREX

"Zyrus has the engineering duty roster," Ryklin informed me as I finished washing up after my shift. We'd been assigned to different parts of the station, so he arrived back to our quarters earlier than usual and had gotten straight to work on the investigation.

"Have you told all of the others?" I asked. More minds might help unravel this puzzle faster, but the six of us weren't all equally adjusted to life outside of the Legion. Thalor and Kyrin especially might pose a problem.

"Just Zyrus. I thought his computer skills might help." He handed me a tablet with a document on the screen, two lines highlighted. "The woman, Pippa, was there as reported. A man named Darian worked it the day before the discovery. The machine only started needing frequent maintenance about two months ago, and Darian was assigned to look at it twice. Pippa was assigned to it four times. The other mechanics listed all only looked at it once."

"Darian is Detyen." I hadn't mentioned our introduction after my dinner with Pippa; I saw no reason to. Something about Darian nagged at me like a burr stuck under my uniform.

"From the Legion?"

"I don't think so. He's younger. He still has his emotions. But there is something ..." I didn't know how to articulate it. "He approached when I had dinner with Pippa. I did not like it when he was at my back." It was difficult to convey feeling without emotion, and we all knew what certain things meant. I couldn't like or dislike anything, not truly, but it got the point across, and Ryklin understood perfectly.

"They warned us that something like that could happen before we consented to this life," Ryklin reminded me.

It was true. There was a lengthy screening process full of warnings and chances to change one's mind before going under the knife and sacrificing your soul. We didn't just stand apart from our brethren, for some of us it was much more serious than that. And it had been years since I'd last encountered a Detyen with his soul intact. My reaction could have been a normal side effect of my condition.

"I will keep that in mind when I speak to him." I didn't want to pollute this investigation with preconceived notions. The soulless were just as susceptible as anyone else, our biases just came from unemotional avenues.

"Perhaps I should instead." Ryklin tapped his fingers against the table, then he looked down at his hand as if he realized what he was doing and flattened it against the surface. "I can give you my opinion of him."

I rejected the suggestion immediately. "No, we need to keep a low profile. He already knows there's one Detyen on the ship, no need to alert him to more. We can't risk the exposure. I will try to record the conversation."

"Very well." Ryklin was a statue again, no nervous gestures. We weren't in the Legion anymore where one non-standard move would see us evaluated and possibly terminated, but the training was deeply ingrained. I had no reason to comment, so I kept my mouth shut.

I put my communicator in my pocket and left our quarters. It wasn't quite mealtime but I could probably catch Darian near the mess hall I'd dined in with Pippa. He might even be eating there with Pippa.

I clenched my teeth, and my hand itched, the talons pricking under my skin with the need to escape.

Why?

I relaxed my jaw and my hands as I waited for the lift. Pippa could eat her meals with whomever she liked; I had no say in the matter. She was just a woman who lived on the station, same as any other. What she did with Darian was none of my business.

My jaw clenched again.

What were these physical responses? It must have something to do with my suspicions about Darian. If he had anything to do with Fran's death, then Pippa could be in danger if she was near him. That made sense. It was logical. It had to be the answer.

I pressed the button for the third level so hard it squeaked under my finger. Once I reached my level, I walked faster than necessary. My vision narrowed on my destination until I could almost feel the kind of focus that only came in the midst of battle.

This was wrong.

I forced myself to stop walking and consider my actions. I was nearly running through the halls like a madman, certainly calling attention to myself. If I met Darian in this state, I wouldn't be objective.

I turned away from the mess hall and headed towards the residential quarters. Fran lived on this floor, and perhaps her room could tell me something that would help. The hallways were wider up here and brighter. There was no overflow of belongings pushed up against the walls, detritus that couldn't fit in cramped quarters.

Two residents passed me by and gave me friendly smiles, which I replied to with a nod. If I had to, I could produce a smile, but it always looked forced.

The six of us could probably afford quarters in an area like this, but it had never come up. My room had been assigned to me when I took the job on the space-scaping crew, and it served its purpose. What would we do with a bigger space? We could sit in silence well enough where we lived now.

Living on a floor like this, with those smiling people, was too much of a risk. No one asked questions on the seventh level. No doubt plenty of people had their secrets, but it was not for me to discover them.

I was here to learn about Fran.

The plate beside her door bore her name, and there was a keypad with a bioscanner. I didn't know her entrance code and certainly couldn't hack the bioscan. I tried the door, just to see if I had a bit of luck.

It was locked.

Not surprising. And not much of a hindrance.

Kyrin was a handyman on the ship and had repaired dozens of doors just like this since arriving on the station, and he'd shown us the trick to bypassing the lock to get a stuck door open. I held down the zero and the five on the keypad along with the ENTER key and waited until the keypad beeped twice before I moved the handle up and down twice. If the door had truly been stuck, all that would do would be to disengage the lock. Since there was no problem with this door, it slid open like I'd entered the correct code.

The entrance to Fran's room was a mess, and it smelled of spoiled food. That was easily explained by the sticky remains of what might have been her dinner strewn across the floor. A chair was knocked on its side, and the table beside the entrance was broken.

I stepped through the mess carefully, trying to avoid as much as I could. Fran's personal items were all in disarray, but I didn't see any blood. If not for the food on the floor, I might have assumed that Fran was merely a messy person, but even the messiest person couldn't ignore the smell for long. She would have at least cleaned that up.

What could her room tell me about her final moments?

If there had been any doubt in my mind that she was the woman in the incinerator, it was gone now. Someone had forcibly taken her out of this room. Had she opened the door to her attacker? Or had he, like me, known the way around the lock?

The door rattled, and I realized I hadn't quite closed it all the way. I searched around for somewhere to hide, but the closet was full to bursting, and the bathing quarters were on the other side of the room. There was nowhere for me to go, and I froze, unsure of what to do.

The door slid open, and Pippa's glare turned to a look of confusion. "Drex? What are you doing here?"

9

PIPPA

DREX WAS STANDING in the middle of Fran's quarters with an almost guilty look on his face. His expression was as blank as always, but there was something in the tilt of his eyebrows that made me think he was sorry to be there. Or sorry he got caught.

I'd spent the day wracking my brain trying to figure out who might have had Fran's entry code in the hopes that I could get into her room and take a peek. A quickly shrinking part of me had hoped I'd find her in there, maybe sick in bed with some nasty flu so she'd been unable to open the door to my knocking.

When I saw the door opened a crack, hope had bloomed for just a second. And then it all came crashing down when I saw Drex.

Disappointment wasn't something I wanted to associate with the man.

"Drex?" I prompted again when he didn't answer me.

"Close the door," he commanded.

I obeyed automatically, only realizing that maybe I shouldn't have when I heard the lock click shut. Drex had been right there when I got locked into G-man. He'd been the first one there after I found Fran's remains. And now he was in her room, a room I was certain had been locked the night before.

Could Drex have something to do with this?

Everything in me rebelled at the thought. Drex was—Okay, I didn't know what Drex was like. Not really. One dinner and some steamy thoughts and bad poetry didn't make a love match. But I knew to the depths of my soul that he was a good guy. My heart rate wasn't spiking. I didn't feel the need to back up or run. My brain might be trying to warn me, but my body wasn't the tiniest bit worried.

"Why are you in Fran's quarters?" I asked. "How did you get in here?"

"I used the override code," he explained, tone calm. As if that was a totally okay thing to do. "It's how the station's handymen open up doors when they're stuck. And I thought I would come in here to see if I could find any information about Fran's death."

I knew I should be more concerned about him being in here, but I couldn't. "You believe me?" He'd held me while I cried in front of Fran's door. Had that only been last night? After little sleep and a day spent trying to come up with avenues of investigation when I had few resources and no skills at this kind of thing, I was a frayed wire ready to snap at the slightest tension.

"Of course." He said it as if believing me was the most obvious thing in the world. "Station security didn't seem motivated to look into this, so I'm doing it myself."

I lunged forward, wrapping my arms tight around him and holding on like he was my only lifeline. "Thank you." It was almost a sob. Under me, Drex stiffened, every muscle locked tight.

Oh.

I loosened my grip and let go, stepping back and putting a meter of space between us. "Thank you," I said again, voice steadier. "How can I help?"

His eyes flashed for a moment. Was that red? How did they do that? But before I could be sure of what I'd seen, they were back to black. "I ... appreciate the offer," he said as if the word was unfamiliar on his tongue, "but I can handle this on my own. There is no need to trouble yourself."

"Trouble myself? Fran was my coworker. I almost died the same way she did. I need to be involved." She deserved justice. And I needed answers if I was ever going to get a full night's sleep again.

But Drex was adamant. "You are too emotionally entangled in this. Investigation requires objectivity. You do not have that."

"Excuse me?" I couldn't believe what I was hearing. Was this guy serious? "Are you telling me that I'm too emotional? Seriously?" My voice threatened to rise, but I held onto control with a vise grip. I wouldn't prove him right.

He didn't answer immediately, taking a moment to choose his words carefully. Perhaps he was afraid the emotional woman in front of him might fly into a rage. "You are too close to this," he explained, voice infuriatingly calm. "Doctors do not operate on their loved ones when it can be avoided, police do not investigate crimes committed against their family. This is not specific to you. I would say the same to anyone with such a close connection."

I was speechless. Drex was looking at me as if he

was waiting for me to agree, like he'd just cast some sort of magic spell full of logic that would make me bow to his expertise.

"Are you some kind of investigator then?" I asked. "You told me you work on the landscaping crew."

"I had basic training before I came here," he acknowledged. "I wasn't always a landscaper."

"What were you before?" I was angry at the way he'd dismissed me, but it couldn't banish my curiosity or the way heat simmered deep in my gut every time he was near. I wanted to know every-thing there was to know about this man and then discover even more at his side. It was insane, the way the want washed over me. I would have already walked away from any other man.

But Drex had me rooted in place.

He didn't answer my question. Instead, he nodded at the mess in Fran's room. "What's wrong with this place?"

He was deflecting, but by deflecting, he wasn't trying to stop me from investigating. I'd take the win now and push for more later. I took a moment to study the room around me. "I wouldn't think Fran was this messy. And what's that smell?" I sniffed a few times and wrinkled my nose. Yuck.

"Food on the floor," he gestured to my feet.

I looked down and noticed the crusty remnants of dinner that I was standing in. I gingerly stepped farther into the room. "It looks like there was a fight. Or she had a rager and trashed the place. My friend Noelle said she heard loud noises in the hallway the other night. We both live just a few doors down."

Drex took the information in. He prowled around the room, examining everything from the side table beside her bed to the back of a picture she had hanging on the wall. Looking for clues, I supposed. But this wasn't a game, and I was pretty sure her attacker hadn't bothered to leave hints behind the decorations.

Since Drex wasn't kicking me out, I joined him in snooping. I didn't know what I was looking for, but I wasn't sure that mattered. I headed to her food prep area and saw a plate of food sitting beside the cleaning unit. "I think she was eating with some-one," I told Drex. "There's a dirty plate in here."

"It could have been from an older meal," he suggested.

I didn't think so. "It looks like the same stuff that's all over the front entryway. Spaghetti and mystery protein. This plate's barely touched." I wasn't sure what I was supposed to do next. Take a picture? Bag it up? I didn't have anything I could use to preserve the thing, nor did I have a DNA scanner or anything like that. Not that it would do much good; it wasn't like I had any bioscan data to match it to.

Drex came over, face a mask of concentration, and I couldn't look away from him. I was supposed to be focusing on the evidence in front of me, but I was caught in his snare. He pulled something out of his pocket, and that shocked me out of the spell.

"Where'd you get that?" I asked. Handheld medscanners weren't cheap and, besides that, I didn't think there was anywhere you could purchase one on the station. The medic offices had them under lock and key and, as far as I knew, they never left the treatment rooms.

"I borrowed it." Drex held it over the food and moved it in a circle, scanning the rim of the plate. "If there's any biodata, I may be able to pick it up."

"Who'd you borrow it from? If the medic unit finds out you'll be in deep—"

He cut me off. "I didn't borrow it from the medic unit. And the person I borrowed it from gave me permission. No need to worry." He pressed a few buttons on the scanner. "It's analyzing. It may take a while."

"Tell me when you know." I didn't make it a question. If it was a question, he could refuse me. If it was a question, he was in charge here and had some sort of authority. But Drex was just a guy. A tall, sexy, devilishly handsome blue alien that was going to haunt my dreams for years to come, but he wasn't station security. He wasn't anyone official.

He didn't get to box me out.

"Let me do this for you," he said. He stepped close, so close it wouldn't take any effort for me to lean in and find out what he tasted like. The rest of the room faded into nothing, and all there was was him. I wanted so badly to reach out and touch him that my fingers ached with need.

For you.

It was, perhaps, the strangest romantic gesture anyone had ever made for me. Then again, I'd never been anywhere near a murder before.

But I couldn't let him do this alone.

"Tell me when the scan comes back," I repeated.

"Let me escort you back to your room." It wasn't quite an answer, but it wasn't a no either.

"Okay." I hated to leave Fran's room as we found it. She deserved more respect than that, but if station security decided to ever get off their asses and investigate, they'd need to see the state of this place.

In the hall, Drex closed the door and hit a few buttons on the keypad.

"Does the lock override work on every door?" I shuddered. What little sleep I'd been getting was probably the last I'd have for a while if anyone could get inside my room.

"It's disabled in high level security rooms. There may be a different override, but low-level maintenance doesn't know it. But if you engage the mechanical lock as well as the digital one, the override won't be enough to open the door." His voice was even, as always.

What would it take to rile the guy up?

We'd taken a few steps away from Fran's room when someone turned the corner and started coming our way. I smiled as I realized it was Darian and gave him a wave. Beside me, Drex felt like a glacier, staring at Darian as if he were a ship that dared to enter his waters.

Or maybe my brain was being a bit fanciful.

"What are you doing up here?" I asked. "Noelle said you were on a long shift today." With Fran gone and me forced to take the day off, everyone else was working overtime to make up for the short staffing.

"I'm on a break," he said. His gaze flicked to Drex and then back to me. "Still hanging out with your new friend?"

"Clearly." I wasn't positive, but it felt like the air beside me moved, and Drex shifted a few centimeters closer. I didn't like Darian's tone, as if he had some say in who I hung out with. Drex and I hadn't kissed, and we weren't having sex. And even if we did, it was still none of Darian's business.

I kept the smile on my face the whole time. Fran's quarters had shaken me up, and I was on edge and reading extra meaning into everything. Darian probably didn't mean anything by it.

"Were you coming to find Noelle?" I asked. Darian didn't live on this floor, and we were in a residential area. There wasn't a reason for someone who didn't live here to be in this hallway.

"You, actually. I was coming to see how you're holding up. And to ask if you wanted to get dinner." He gave me a hopeful smile.

Drex's shoulder brushed against mine.

"I'm good, really," I insisted before Darian could say anything else. "And not tonight for dinner. Maybe tomorrow. I'll be back to work tomorrow. We'll see." I wasn't exactly sure why I didn't want to agree to anything with Drex standing next to me, and I wasn't going to think too hard about it.

Darian just gave a polite nod. "Got it. Tomorrow." He leaned in and kissed my cheek before turning back the way he came.

"Are you in a relationship with him?" Drex asked once Darian was gone.

I snorted. "Not even a little. Darian doesn't really do relationships. And I'm not interested, even if he was." Darian was the playboy of the engineering crew, and I had no desire to be another notch in his belt. "He's a friend."

Drex rested his hand lightly on the small of my back and guided me the rest of the way to my room.

Once we were there, we stood in front of the locked door, but neither of us made a move. I tilted my head to look up into his onyx eyes. "It means a lot that you're looking into this."

"This is our home. It needs to be safe." He raised his hand and brushed his fingers against my cheek. And his eyes did that strange thing again, flashing an impossible red for only a moment. His brow furrowed, but he didn't pull away. "You need to be safe."

I leaned into his touch. "Not just me."

There was a magnetic pull between us.

Completely impossible to resist. And I didn't want to. I leaned forward until I could brush my lips against his. He froze for a moment, lips tense and unmoving. But then he responded, angling his head and deepening the kiss.

It was perfect. Everything a first kiss was supposed to be.

Until Drex made an anguished sound in the back of his throat and collapsed, unconscious.

10

DREX

MY HEAD ACHED as if someone was taking a pickax to my temple, everything throbbing. I came to slowly and could feel hands gently brushing through my hair and realized my head was cradled in someone's lap.

Certainly not Ryklin or one of my men.

The thought was fleeting, and too trivial for me to focus on. Not when the hands in my hair felt so good. Even if lightning bolts of pain followed their path exactly.

I opened my eyes and looked up to see Pippa, worry clear on her face. The emotion was easier to read than I'd ever experienced since becoming soulless. That was important, I was sure, but I didn't know why.

I'd kissed her.

I'd needed to do it more than I needed my next breath.

It made no sense. I had sacrificed desire along with everything else when I made the decision to serve my people beyond my allotted thirty years.

But the combination of Darian staring at her like he had a claim on her and the thought that she could have been taken away before I knew she existed had been too much. And then she'd touched me.

Agony. Even now, it was acid in my veins wherever we connected, skin to skin. When her fingertips brushed against my forehead, it felt like a knife drawing a pattern. But I didn't pull away. I remembered the ecstasy of that one moment when our lips touched.

I wanted more.

Need pounded within me, and it was finally enough to make me sit up and pull away.

There was only one thing this could be.

Fixation.

It was something that happened to some soulless warriors. We found a person and focused on them to the exclusion of everything else. I'd heard stories of fixations ending in murder and suicide, of bodies piled five high when the blaster shots finally ended and the fixated soulless was put down.

The longer I stayed with her, the more of a risk I was. I needed to leave this room right now, to go back to my quarters, pack a bag, and get off the station. Distance might save her while I deteriorated.

I didn't move.

"We're in my quarters," Pippa said. "You kind of collapsed against me, and I managed to get you inside. I, uh, I used your medscanner." She held it out to me. "It says nothing's wrong with you. You've only been out for a couple of minutes."

I took the scanner and put it in my pocket without looking at the screen. Fixation wouldn't show up; there was nothing physical to diagnose. This problem was completely psychological. "You didn't call a med team?"

She shook her head. "You don't strike me as the kind of guy who wants to go to the medbay. Or come to the attention of anyone official on the station."

Was it that obvious? Outside of my fellow soulless, Pippa was the person I'd willingly spent the most time with on the station. My co-workers didn't count. I spoke to them only when absolutely necessary and always about work. I doubted many of them even knew my name.

But in three days, Pippa already knew more about me than anyone, and I hadn't even had to tell her most of it. We gave up so much when we sacrificed our emotions. I doubted I could have made the inferences she had.

"Thank you, a med team is unnecessary. I would only be taking up space in the medbay. I don't need a medic." What I needed to do was get up.

Instead, I reached for Pippa's hand. It hurt enough to make me gasp as I laced our fingers together. It was a warning, a sign I needed to back off and report my defect. But the longer I held on, the more control I got over the pain until it was barely more than a minor discomfort.

I'd been a soldier once. I was trained to push through things that would destroy a lesser man. A little pain was nothing.

I stared at our joined hands. Her skin was so strange next to mine, that yellowy-beige that humans came in. They varied from light to dark, I knew, and I'd seen the whole spectrum in my travels. A dark clan marking wrapped around my middle finger, and Pippa rubbed at it with the thumb of her other hand.

"Do you know what happened?" Pippa asked. She didn't stop rubbing her thumb against my finger, and my body was flaring to life, pinpricks of pain and something I couldn't name raging through my veins.

I knew I should lie. I should make up a story about needing to eat or getting over a vague illness. She didn't need to worry. And she couldn't know. But I couldn't make the lie form on my tongue. "No," I said. "That's never happened before."

"I can't say a kiss from me has ever made a guy pass out before." She gave me a rueful smile. "I know the medscanner says you're fine, but you really should have a medic check you out. Just in case. People don't just pass out for no reason."

I focused on her lips as she formed the words, and I couldn't look away. The shape, the color, the fullness that made them so fascinating. No one had ever said how close fixation came to true emotion. I could only remember the echoes of what it meant to feel, but those echoes were screaming in my head now so loud they drowned out everything else.

"It's not something physical," I assured her.

I didn't realize my answer was a mistake until she pounced. "So, you do know what happened?"

I wasn't going to lie to her. The realization was

strong within my gut. But the secret of my soulless-ness wasn't mine to tell, not alone. I had five other men depending on me keeping our status hidden. And the soulless were the most classified and shameful project the Detyen Legion had ever under-taken. The Legion had cast me aside and left me for dead, but I the instinct to protect my people ran deep.

But I had to say something.

"I have a condition that makes emotion ... diffi-cult," I said, and even that felt like a lie. But I didn't have the words to tell her that a medic had sliced into my brain and scrambled things until I'd never again be the man I once was. "I suspect that ..." I couldn't finish.

Pippa caught on. "You like me so much it made you pass out?" There was a hint of disbelief in her voice, but she didn't pull away. "That's not so bad, is it?"

She sat there with open trust on her face, her lips kissable, and her hands wrapped up with mine. Every second I sat with her would only make the fixation worse. If I couldn't protect myself, I had to protect her. I pulled my hand away and stood. "I need to leave. You can't ... We can't ... This can go no further."

Pippa scrambled to her feet and wedged herself between me and the door. "What's going on, Drex?"

"Please move." I had to shut down whatever the fixation was doing to me. And I had to get off Nebula Outpost.

But how could I leave when Fran's killer was still on the loose and Pippa might still be at risk?

"I need to return to my quarters," I said. "I can't do this."

She studied my face for several seconds before giving me a solemn nod and stepping aside. I hurried out of the room before either of us could say anything else.

I had to end this. Before it was too late for both of us.

11

PIPPA

Two days. Two endless freaking days of work and fear and boredom and not a sign of Drex. I yanked the screwdriver a bit too tight, and my shoulder jerked as the laws of physics punished me for failing to pay attention. I glared at the fitting and moved onto the next one. The machine was back in working order, and once I had this panel fitted, my shift would be over.

Then I could go wallow some more.

"Ugh, come on, girl!" I was thankful no one else was around to hear me give myself a pathetic little pep talk.

Drex didn't owe me anything. It was one *fleeting* kiss and a bit of hand holding. What was I, thirteen?

If he didn't want to take it further than that, I couldn't make him.

But it felt like I was missing a giant chunk of information. What kind of condition would make it so he couldn't feel his emotions and he fainted from a kiss? Nothing I could look up on the Nebula Outpost databanks, that was for sure. And nothing I'd seen from him suggested he didn't feel. Sure, he was kind of reserved, but he'd been nothing but kind to me.

Or maybe that was just cold politeness, and I was reading too far into this thing.

I didn't know if he was still looking into Fran's disappearance. I didn't have his comm data to send him a message, and sending one through the station's messaging system seemed like asking for trouble. I wasn't going to march down to his room and demand answers.

First of all, his roommate gave me the creeps. If anyone was emotionless, it was him. Second of all, I refused to chase. Drex said nothing could happen between us, and I would respect that. But I wouldn't stop him from coming back and changing his mind.

Did that make me pathetic?

I leaned forward and knocked my head against

the machine, and the cool metal did nothing to solve my problems.

I had to put Drex out of my mind.

Who killed Fran?

That didn't do much to banish him. The last bit of investigation I'd done into the whole thing involved him breaking into her quarters. Had he managed to get any data off the plate? I wondered if there was any security footage in the hallway that might give a clue as to her attacker or whatever had happened that night.

Not likely. I knew the security feeds got wiped every few days, and they were monitored by an algorithm instead of real people. If the algorithm didn't flag anything as suspicious, the data was long gone. Besides, only station security would have access to that, and I didn't have a way to get close.

But I had the duty roster. And I hadn't spoken to Darian about the situation yet.

I sat back and packed up my things. My mood was grim but determined, and at least I had a path forward. I needed to find Darian and see what he knew about Fran or if he'd seen anything weird.

He wasn't in the engineering locker room or break room when I locked up my things. I checked the duty roster hanging on the wall and saw that he'd been assigned to look at the heating system over in B-quadrant on the fourth level, and he wasn't due to get off shift for another hour.

I could wait for him in the break room and offer to take him to dinner. We hadn't seen each other in a couple of days, despite my promise to get a meal with him. But the thought of waiting for more than an hour had me antsy. If I headed over to 4B right away, Darian would likely be finishing up right as I arrived, and we could talk on the way back.

It didn't occur to me that he might not have anything to say until I was halfway there, but at that point, I was committed.

Unfortunately, by the time I made it to 4B, Darian was nowhere to be seen.

Damn it. I should have just waited.

If I returned to the locker room, he'd be long gone by the time I made it back. I didn't want to chase him through the station all night, and it wasn't like he was going anywhere. I could talk to him another day. Our shifts were likely to match up soon; we usually worked together at least once a week.

The lifts were at the other end of 4B, but there was an access ladder up to the third floor at the end of the hallway. It would dump me in a storage hallway that was always super dark and cramped, but it would save me fifteen minutes of walking.

I shimmied through the hatch and grabbed onto the metal rung of the ladder that was bolted to the side of the wall. I wished they could selectively turn off gravity on these ladders; it would make climbing a lot easier. But it would make maintenance hell. I shuddered to consider what a station with gravity differentials like that would need in maintenance. It might tear itself apart.

The hatch to the third floor opened without the tiniest hint of a sound. Someone was staying on top of keeping the hinges lubricated. Good for them. That got overlooked all the time.

The third floor's storage room was crammed with every bit of detritus that had collected over the years that hadn't been destroyed or repurposed into something else. Throwing things away wasn't something we did easily on a station this far away from anywhere. There was no telling when we could get replacements for what we needed. So, we repaired things endlessly and recycled and repurposed. And we stored. Holy hell, did we store things.

Space wasn't as much of an issue as people expected it to be. It might have been a problem if we were launching from down on Nebula, but building on extra sections to the stations in our orbital position was simple enough. So, when we needed more storage, or in the past when we needed more rooms for people to sleep, the station grew.

The population was dwindling these days with the mine on Nebula long closed, but that just gave us room for more stuff.

I gingerly made my way through the narrow walkway between two rows of things. Most were packaged in crates or wrapped in tarps, and the curious part of me wanted to pause to explore. Maybe if I'd satisfied my investigative urges by interrogating Darian, I wouldn't be so tempted, but it was like thousands of birthday gifts were wrapped up all around me, and I wanted to tear them open.

I kept my hands to myself as I made it to the exit.

The hallway outside was empty. The storage areas of the station always felt a bit dead.

I headed towards my quarters, but after a minute, the back of my neck prickled like I was being watched. I jerked my head back, but no one was behind me. It was just me and my echoing footsteps.

But I sped up anyway, walking so fast some might have called it a jog. My heart rate kicked up, and sweat prickled on my neck. I was sure someone was watching me, was coming for me. And if I could just get back to my room, I'd be safe.

It was like my nightmares had come to life and were trying to claw me down into the darkness that had haunted my sleep for the past week. This wasn't real, it couldn't be. My anxiety and paranoia were playing tricks on me, and nothing was out there to hurt me.

Except someone had hurt Fran. And maybe they'd also tried to kill me.

My walk turned into an all-out sprint.

Then the lights went out.

I knew the path back to my room by heart, but before I could turn down the next hallway and find light, something crashed into my side and slammed me against the wall. I yelped in pain and struggled to get away, but whoever was there was bigger and stronger.

One hand clamped over my mouth, blocking my air and the scream that tried to escape my throat. Some demonic instinct possessed me, and I licked the palm of the hand, flicking my tongue out and tasting salty skin. The hand jerked back as if burned, and I punched blindly, connecting with something that made my attacker grunt.

But the lights were out, and I couldn't see a

damn thing. I kicked out, but didn't connect. I punched again, and this time the shadow that was my assailant dodged. That was all I needed. Their grip loosened just enough that I managed to yank myself loose and sprint blindly towards my room.

Tears streamed down my face, my uniform had to be askew, and my throat hurt enough that I suspected it would turn black and blue before long.

The lights of the next hallway were nearly blinding, and I squinted against them and didn't stop until I made it in front of my quarters. I tried to punch in my entry code, but the tears in my eyes blurred my vision, and my hand shook so much that I couldn't get the numbers right.

A shadow crossed over my shoulder, and I flinched, sure that my end had come to get me. I spun around, and for a second, the sight of blue skin and dark hair made me think it was Drex.

But it was his roommate. Ryklin.

"What happened?" Ryklin asked in the same infuriatingly even tone that Drex sometimes used.

I opened my mouth to say something, but my throat was raw, and the tears turned into a sob. I wished he was Drex so I could throw my arms around him and let him take some of my worries away.

There was no way in hell I'd ever hug Ryklin.

His eyes flicked up and down, taking me in. "Were you attacked?"

I managed a nod.

"Do you know who attacked you?" he asked, voice infuriatingly calm.

I shook my head. It had been so dark, and I couldn't tell the species of my attacker or their gender. And with the lights out, there was no hope of security footage.

"Fr ... Fran." It was a weak whisper of a word, but Ryklin nodded. Drex must have told him about the investigation because he didn't ask any questions about who or what I could mean.

"Pippa?" Noelle's voice echoed down the hallway as she ran towards us. She got in front of Ryklin and pulled me close. "Oh, my gods, what happened to you?"

"She needs medical attention," Ryklin said, backing up a step to clear the way for my friend. "Would you like me to call the medical team?"

I shook my head; I didn't need that. I wasn't that hurt. "Tea," I said. It was barely a rasp.

Noelle gave Ryklin an assessing look. "Did you see her attacker?" she asked. Her voice was calm too, but the calm that came before a storm, all fury and potential barely caged.

"No, she must have fought him off. I found her here. And I will leave you to tend her." He paused and then continued. "If you require my statement to make a report to station security, she knows where to find me."

Noelle ushered me into the room and got me set up on my couch before she made two cups of tea. She did it all in silence, worry written across her face. A few sips of tea soothed my throat, and judging by the slightly medicinal taste to the brew, she probably put a bit of healing serum in it. I wasn't going to complain.

"Do you want to report the attack?" Noelle asked. "What if ..." She trailed off.

But I'd been thinking the same thing. "It could have been the same person who killed Fran."

"Yeah," she sighed. "I mean, how many psycho killers can there be on the ship?"

Despite the pain in my throat and the throbbing in my head, I laughed.

She opened her mouth to say something, but her communicator chimed with an appointment reminder. She pulled it out and cursed. "My family is scheduled to call. Let me just postpone this. It'll be alright."

"Don't. Take the call. I'm fine." Live calls from across the galaxy were expensive and difficult to coordinate. It could be weeks or longer before Noelle managed to talk to someone from home. "I'll stay in my room," I promised. "It's okay."

Her face scrunched up, clearly conflicted. But she relented. "Okay, but I know this makes me a terrible friend, and don't tell me otherwise."

"But it makes you a good daughter."

She hugged me and kissed my forehead before leaving me alone. I drank the tea and was almost feeling okay, wrung out from all the adrenaline, but surviving. I would be okay. No one could get to me in my room.

There was a knock at the door.

No way was it Noelle; she'd be talking for at least an hour. Fear and something like anticipation buzzed in my veins. I checked the peephole, and relief washed through me.

I opened the door and collapsed into Drex's arms.

12

DREX

Pippa's chest heaved with sobs as I moved us farther into her quarters and let the door slide shut behind me. I gripped her tight, even as a wave of pain washed over my own body.

The past two days had done nothing to ease the fixation, and the moment Ryklin had told me what happened to her, I came running. He'd have something to say about that, no doubt. But Pippa was all that mattered.

I managed to get us to the couch and eased Pippa down, sitting beside her. She leaned against me, and I was unsure of what to do. I didn't have words of comfort. If there was any hope of hunting down the person who'd hurt her, I'd do it without hesitation. But to do that, I'd need to ask her about what happened, and she was in no state to talk.

I started to run my fingers through her hair, gently easing through the tangles. It was soothing, even for me. And my skin didn't burn as much this time when we touched. I didn't know if that was a good or bad thing. The pain was a reminder that I shouldn't be doing this. But since I refused to walk away, it was a useless nuisance.

After several minutes, Pippa quieted, and she pulled back just enough that she could look at my face. I still stroked her hair, unable to stop touching her. I'd never been physically affectionate, not even before I lost my soul, but with Pippa I couldn't pull away.

"I'm getting your shirt all splotchy," she muttered.

"It can be washed." A damp shirt was the least of my concerns.

"Nebula Outpost is supposed to be safe." She said it defiantly, as if daring me to contradict her.

I didn't know how to respond. The facts were becoming clear. She'd been attacked. Another woman was dead. Something was clearly amiss, and Pippa might be a target rather than a random victim.

Heat seared through me, and my claws threatened to flare out at the invisible enemy.

Pippa sucked in a ragged breath. "Your eyes ..."

"What?" I looked down at her, my gaze snared in hers. Her eyes were soft and full of emotion, fear and anger and something I couldn't read but knew was just for me.

"They turn red sometimes. I've never seen that before." She lifted her hand and slowly traced a finger over my cheekbone, resting her hand on my face.

There was the pain again, stabbing needle pricks telling me I needed to back away.

I leaned into the touch. "They shouldn't do that." It had to be another sign of fixation, though I'd never heard of it. Normal Detyen eyes turned red when we experienced strong emotion. As one of the soulless, I couldn't feel anything. And yet, the longer I sat beside Pippa, the more that felt like a lie.

"Is it an implant?" she asked. She hadn't stopped stroking my face.

"No. These are the eyes I was born with." I covered her hand with my palm. "It's you."

"Me?" She swallowed, and I stared at the way her throat bobbed.

"I shouldn't be like this." I didn't know how to

tell her what I meant, and I knew I shouldn't say anything at all. I should have been light years away from Nebula Outpost by now, but Pippa was a star whose gravity I was caught in. There was no escape.

"Like what?" she asked.

I kissed her.

It was gentler than before, and a distant part of me was aware that this might end the same way as it had last time, with me unconscious and completely dependent on Pippa for protection. But though there was a pounding pain in my head, there was no wave of blackness coming to swallow me whole.

And Pippa responded, leaning into me and letting her tongue trace against the seam of my lips until I opened for her. Her tongue darted into my mouth, and a thousand stars exploded within me.

Desire.

It had been missing from my life since I woke up in the medbay with wires attached to my body and a hollow place where my emotions should have been. But with Pippa in my arms, it came rushing back, burning hotter than a sun.

I could lose myself in the kiss forever. I laced my fingers through her hair and groaned against her mouth, pleasure raging within me.

This couldn't be true. Soulless warriors didn't feel desire or anything else. There was no road back, no salvation.

But in her arms, I was almost the man I used to be.

If this was fixation, I could see why my brethren went mad and refused to give it up. How could I when I finally wanted after so long? How could I when the answer to all the dreams I'd given up was safe in my arms?

Pippa shifted her position until she was straddling my thighs, and I groaned again. She brushed against my cock, and sensation roared through me. I wasn't hard, not yet. But I could be.

Erections were another uncommon sensation. My body could still produce them, blood still flowed as it should, but they were an annoyance.

There was nothing annoying about what she was making me feel.

She ground against me, and I broke the kiss, pressing my lips to her cheek, her jaw, her neck. She tasted sweet, and I dragged my tongue along her skin until I reached the spot where her pulse raced. I grazed my teeth against her flesh, sucking lightly, marking her as my own.

This had to be the madness of fixation. I had no

claim to her. She wasn't my woman, couldn't be my denya. Detyens recognized their mates on sight, and mates were another thing sacrificed in becoming soulless.

But for now, she was mine. It was so easy to pretend with Pippa in my lap and her taste on my tongue.

A part of me thought that I should pull back, that we might take things to a place Pippa would regret. But she kissed me with a desperate fervor that was impossible to resist, and I hadn't needed to practice resisting temptation in years. I had no defenses against her.

I wanted none.

No, from her I wanted more. Wanted everything.

My fingers found the hem of her shirt, and I explored, stroking my palms against her waist and back, teasing beneath her breasts. I wanted to tear off the layers of fabric separating us, but already I could feel static in the back of my mind, a dark fuzziness that warned I was reaching my limit.

I pulled back. Pippa had been through enough. She didn't need an unconscious man on her sofa.

But I kept kissing her, clutching her close. If she was disappointed I didn't take it further, she didn't mention it. Slowly, she pulled back, though not before taking a few more lingering kisses. Her skin was flushed, eyes bright.

"Your eyes are red again," she said.

No surprise there. Not anymore. I didn't say anything.

Pippa leaned against me. "Please don't go."

"I'm not going anywhere." Not tonight. Not ever. If there was a moment for me to escape this fixation, it had passed. Wherever this was going, I was going to see it through.

And no matter how it ended, I was going to ensure Pippa made it out. There was no hope for me, but I could give her the future I'd never had.

It was the least I could do.

13
PIPPA

MY QUARTERS HAD NEVER FELT SO small until Drex came to them. Or perhaps I was just too aware of him. I could have stayed on his lap all night, stealing kisses and hoping for more. But there was a tension to him, and it wasn't the sexy kind. I didn't have a single doubt in my mind that he wanted the kisses just as much as I did.

Wanted. Ha! Kissing him was as necessary as breathing.

But I remembered the terror of our first kiss, the way his body had gone limp, and I'd thought that I'd done something to hurt him. I didn't want a repeat of that.

The only way to ensure I didn't launch myself

right back at him was to keep busy. I spotted the mug that Noelle had put on the table, and lunged for it, springing to my feet and heading for the sink. "Would you like a cup of tea?" I asked. Mine had gone cold, so I dumped it in the sink and programmed the food processor to prepare a fresh cup.

"Yes." Drex remained sitting, eyes black again, and his expression intense. His clothes were a little rumpled, but his posture was as stiff as a fresh soldier's.

I stared for a moment longer before yanking my gaze away and preparing a cup for him. When I took my seat again, I kept a solid distance between us. No more funny business. "I thought I was going to go a little crazy when Noelle left," I said, sipping my tea. It was still a bit too hot, but that was fine.

"Why did she leave you?" His voice was back to that flat tone he normally spoke in. In the heat of the moment, I hadn't realized it had changed at all, and now I missed it.

"A scheduled call back to The Consortium to talk to her family. I told her to go." Drex didn't say anything else, so I found myself telling him about Noelle. She was my closest friend on the station, and

I didn't want him thinking she was the kind of person to abandon someone when they were in pain. "I was assigned to supervise her when she was fresh out of training. From the first sentence, everything just clicked into place. You know how it's just like that with people sometimes?"

His face was grave as he nodded. "Yes."

I swallowed and had to look away. Yeah. It wasn't just Noelle that I clicked with. And I'd never wanted to crawl into her lap and devour her.

"Her family is back in The Consortium; it's super far away. I mean, everything's far from Nebula, but this is even worse. She had a three-year training contract and was supposed to head back home, but she stuck around. I guess this place has a way of sucking people in. What brought you here?" I knew Drex worked in landscaping on the station and that he hadn't always been a landscaper. There were thousands of planets or space stations he could have gone to. Nebula Outpost wasn't exciting, and I doubted most of the wider universe even knew it existed.

He didn't answer, and I wondered if it was a delicate question. Drex had secrets, that was clear. What could make a man appear as cold as ice one moment and cause him to faint when he kissed? What was he running from?

"I was a soldier, once," he finally said when I'd given up hope for a response. "And what I'm about to tell you cannot leave this room. I need your word, Pippa." His face was grave. "You cannot tell Noelle, and certainly not Darian. Not anyone." He reached out and squeezed my hand.

I could barely breathe from the weight of his stare. "Your secrets are safe with me." Maybe I shouldn't have been so quick to agree, but I was eager to know. And I trusted Drex. If he said something was a secret, there was a reason.

"They aren't just my secrets," he warned. "If it was just me ... It's not. Sharing this information is a capital offense."

"Then maybe you shouldn't tell me."

He squeezed my hand again. "I've escaped two death sentences already. I do not fear this."

Okay, I was too intrigued to try and stop him again.

"I am a Detyen, like your friend Darian. As is my roommate, Ryklin."

I nodded. I'd figured that much out myself.

"But unlike Darian, who must have been born in a Detyen settlement somewhere, I was a part of the

Detyen Legion. Do you know anything about that?" He hadn't let go of my hand.

I found myself leaning closer. "No. Darian hasn't told me much about Detyens. I just know that you're blue."

"Not just blue," he corrected. "Gold, green, purple, even red. We come in a variety of hues. Though variations of blue are the most common. But our looks are not the important thing. About a hundred years ago, something destroyed our home planet. The only people to escape were those near enough ships to get off the planet within a few minutes of the destruction or those already off planet. None of that is secret. I was born into the only military unit that escaped that day. We're called the Detyen Legion."

"That's terrible." My heart hurt for people who'd died a century ago, and I thought back to the explosion that had stolen my parents from me. Some wounds never truly healed.

"That's not all."

"There's more?" His planet had been destroyed; what other tragedy did he need?

His face didn't shift as he spoke, no nervous tics, and his voice was as monotone as always. "Yes, unfortunately. Do you know about the Denya Price?"

I shook my head. "What's a denya?"

Drex was quiet for a moment, and he pulled his hand away. "A fated mate. Each Detyen is supposed to have a perfect match."

Just the thought of it gave me a funny feeling in the pit of my stomach. Not bad, just ... weird. "That sounds nice."

"And if we don't find them before the age of thirty, we die."

"Not nice. What the hell?" What kind of devil's bargain was that? I kept that question to myself. Obviously, Drex had no say over how his people evolved.

He didn't react to my outburst. "With so few Detyens left, there were also few mates to find. I can only speak to the Legion; I don't know what Detyens in other settlements do. We found a way to extend our lives at a great price. I agreed to it seven years ago. There are strict behavioral guidelines in place for those of us who undergo this procedure. Those of us who fail to adhere are executed. I was slotted for death but my commanding officer didn't agree with the sentence. He made it appear that I chose to take my own life and got me safely away. The Legion has no reason to come to Nebula Outpost."

Hearing his story made me sick. "What did you

... Why did they sentence you?" Drex had been nothing but kind to me, and I couldn't imagine what rule he would have broken.

He pondered that for a moment. "My unit was on leave. I was the only so—I was the only person who'd undergone the procedure. We were on a small planet near the edge of the Oscavian Empire. I had heard stories of the wildlife on this place as a boy and had always wanted to see it. I was supposed to stay in my quarters. Instead, I took a walk through a wildlife sanctuary on the edge of town. My deviation from orders was too big to be ignored."

"They wanted to kill you for taking a walk?" If I ever found this Detyen Legion, they'd get a piece of my mind. What kind of monsters would execute their own men for something so innocuous?

Drex looked down at his hands. They clutched his mug. He didn't fidget, but I got the impression that he was nervous. "There's a name for people like me, people who undergo the procedure."

I had to bite my tongue to keep from prompting him for more. He was getting there. He just needed time.

"We're called the soulless. I can't give you specific information about what was done to me, not exactly. I don't know what happened. Either something was removed from me or some connection was severed in my mind. It means that my body did not die when I passed my thirtieth birthday, but I could no longer feel emotion. A soulless warrior, one functioning correctly, would have never taken a walk of his own volition, not just because he'd wanted to see the flying snakes he'd read about as a child. That deviation didn't hurt anyone, but one deviation can lead to others."

"You sound as if you agree with your sentence." No emotion. It didn't make sense. A man without emotion couldn't kiss me like Drex did, like he was drowning and I was his oxygen.

"If I agreed with the sentence, I would not have run when I had the chance."

He finished his tea, and I grabbed the mug and put it beside mine on the cleaning tray. I gripped the edge of the counter as I tried to make sense of everything he'd just said. There were probably a million things I should ask, that I should care about, but my mind could only focus on one.

I couldn't face him as I asked. I stared down at the dirty cups and willed my mouth to stay shut, even as the words forced their way out. "If you don't feel emotion, why did you kiss me?"

I heard a whisper of movement, fabric on fabric,

and then felt the heat of his body against my back. His hand rested on my hip before sliding around to hold me close, his head nestled in the crook of my neck. "Because when I'm with you, I remember what it's like to feel."

14

PIPPA

MY MIND WHIRLED with everything Drex had said as I got ready for work. I decided not to tell station security about the attack. I didn't want them distracted from Fran's murder, and it wasn't like I'd been hurt, just shaken up. Drex hadn't liked it at first, but I'd made him understand.

When I'm with you, I remember what it's like to feel.

The words were warmth curled in my belly. It wasn't a declaration of love. And, given all he'd told me, it wasn't like we had a hope for a future. Maybe all we'd ever have was a few stolen kisses and an echo of what could have been.

But he'd stayed the night with me, sleeping on the couch to make sure that my attacker didn't come back. I'd wanted to invite him to my bed, but if kissing me had made him pass out, I didn't know what sleeping next to me might do, and I knew he wouldn't risk it.

"You look happy," Noelle said as she entered the locker room and started to store her stuff. "How? Are you feeling okay?"

Maybe I shouldn't have been but ... "Drex came by last night. We talked." I couldn't say a word about the Detyen Legion or the soulless. Those weren't my secrets to tell.

Before she could make any sort of remark, Darian stuck his head through the door. "You're with me today, Pip. One of the retention tanks is threatening to leak."

"Schedule says I'm doing inventory." I reached for my communicator to double-check and saw a message from the boss about the change in assignment. "Or not. Ugh. Let me change my boots." Living on a space station meant reusing as much as we could, including waste, and the retention tanks held megaliters of nastiness.

Darian was quiet as we made our way to our destination. I snuck a sideways glance at him and wondered if he'd know anything about Drex and his people. But Drex had been adamant that I not say a word about the

Detyen Legion to Darian. That didn't mean I couldn't ask anything. Conversations about differences in our species were an old pastime on a place as diverse as Nebula Outpost. The closer two species appeared, the more fun it was to find out our idiosyncrasies.

"How are you doing?" Darian asked. He was more subdued today than normal.

"Did Noelle tell you?" I hadn't told her to keep the attack quiet, but she should have known I didn't want it spread around.

"Tell me what?" He took a step in front of me and turned around, blocking my path. "What happened? Are you alright?"

Oh. So, he'd been asking in general. "It's nothing; I'm fine."

"It doesn't sound like nothing."

I could have deflected, but I didn't want to lie to my friend. "Someone attacked me last night when I was walking home." I'd slept with the lights on, and Drex hadn't said a word about it. I doubted I'd sleep in full dark for a long time.

"What? When? Are you okay?" He reached for me.

I took a step back; I didn't need comfort now, and I didn't want to cry on Darian's shoulder. "I'm fine. I punched him and managed to get away. I don't want to talk about it."

Darian's jaw tightened. "Did you tell security?"

"No. It was too dark to see anything—no gender, no species, nothing. And the cameras wouldn't have caught anything. I want them focusing on Fran, not me." I took a step forward, and Darian relented, falling into step beside me.

"You should have called me," he said. "I would have come and helped."

"Noelle was there. And Drex. I'm okay, I promise." Even Ryklin was there, but I didn't mention him. I didn't think Darian knew who he was, anyway. I hadn't thought much about it last night, but why was he outside my quarters?

"Seems like I was the only one not invited to the party." His voice turned sour.

I had to suppress a scowl. "I'm sorry, the next time a stranger assaults me in a dark hallway, you'll be the first one I call." I could still feel the grip of malevolent hands, and the shadows seemed to move whenever I stared at them for too long.

"Fuck, you're right. I'm sorry. You're my friend. I'm allowed to worry, aren't I?"

"Of course." But why did he have to make my assault about himself? Maybe I was being unfair.

"You and Drex seem to be getting close." He grinned at me and any tension seemed to slip off his face.

"He's nice." I didn't want to share anything that went on between Drex and I with Darian; it felt too private. I didn't even want to tell Noelle everything that I could, not yet. I wanted to protect it, to keep it just between the two of us. But now that I knew a bit more about Detyens, I did have a question. "How old are you, Darian?"

The smile dropped off his face. "You meet a second Detyen and suddenly you're asking that?"

"I've known you for years and realized I didn't know. I'm just curious." We'd never celebrated his birthday. Maybe Detyens didn't. Or maybe it was just Darian.

He sighed. "I'm twenty-eight. I'm not about to drop dead on you, if that's what you're worried about." He scowled as he said it.

If I didn't know about the Denya Price, I'd be really confused by that. I needed to steer this conversation in another direction. "I was thinking about G-man the other day."

"Yeah?" Just like that, his mood changed. "What about? Other than his sudden hunger for tasty human ladies."

I glared. "What the hell, dude?"

"Too soon?" He winced.

I wanted to punch him in the arm for that. "Yes. The heat death of the universe will be too soon for that joke. I was locked inside that thing." I shuddered and had to swallow down a bit of bile before I could suppress the urge to barf.

He scrunched up his face. "I'm sorry. You're right. That was shitty."

"As I was saying." I frowned at him. "I think you worked on G-man right before I did. Did you notice anything weird? Or maybe anyone lurking around? Anything that might give us a clue as to what happened?" It was possible that what had happened to me was merely a mechanical malfunction, a terrifying accident that could have happened to anyone. But Fran's end was no accident.

Darian thought for a moment. "I think I saw another Detyen, not your new friend." There was a biting emphasis on that word. "Maybe twice over the last month, he was jogging through the sector while I was working on the machine. I also saw *your* Detyen down there once. It's not a restricted area, but those are the only non-maintenance people I ever saw."

"You don't know the other Detyens on the ship?"

I asked. I was right about Ryklin, then. And Drex had mentioned others.

"Could you name all the humans?" he countered.

Good point. Maybe. As far as I knew, Drex and his people were the only other Detyens on Nebula Outpost. But they had every reason to stay far away from Darian.

I wondered what Ryklin had been doing around G-man. He couldn't have been the one to attack me the night before, not with how fast I'd run from my attacker to get to my room. But that didn't mean that something wasn't up.

I'd have to give Ryklin a closer look. Drex trusted his people. But was that trust misplaced?

15
DREX

Ryklin had me under observation. I may not have noticed if Zyrus hadn't been staring at me for the last five minutes. It shouldn't have mattered. Nothing did.

But that wasn't the case anymore. Not since Pippa.

"Have you made any headway into finding security footage?" I asked him. He'd been a technology specialist in the Legion, and with the right equipment, he'd even hacked into the highest security servers in the Oscavian Empire once or twice. Now he was a janitor.

"There's nothing from the victim's residence hallway nor from the corridor near the incinerator," he reported. "It's been wiped. I'm analyzing the logs to see if that was automatic or if someone came to do it on purpose."

"So, we have no security footage." Pippa would be crushed.

"I did not say that," Zyrus corrected. "There may be something along the path between the two points we know our person of interest was at. I have collected all of the footage that I can and have an algorithm analyzing it for activity. Unless the perpetrator knows of every camera on the station or has direct access to the feeds, it's unlikely they could wipe all the footage. If they were the ones to erase it, of course."

It was something. "I see. Keep me updated."

"Of course." Zyrus continued to sit there in silence.

The need to do something thrummed in me, and I was tempted to pace. Tempted. I wasn't supposed to be tempted by anything, but the ghost of Pippa's lips on mine was proof enough that some temptations could overcome the impossible.

What would Ryklin do if he found out what had happened between Pippa and I? No force in the galaxy could pry the words from my lips, but I could already feel my emotionless walls crumbling.

The six of us soulless outcasts didn't have a

leader. We were from different units and had been cast aside for different reasons. I had never asked Zyrus what made his superiors decide he was defective. It didn't matter. We had all decided to survive, and there was no use dwelling on the past.

But we all knew that something could still go wrong, that we had to monitor one another for signs of degeneration. And we all knew what needed to be done if one of us crossed that invisible line.

Who would make the decision? Ryklin knew me best, and he'd known something was off for days. He'd seen the way I sprinted from the room when he told me of the attack on Pippa. Perhaps he was too close to me and would be reluctant to put me down. Zyrus was the most calculating among us, and he might take the decision out of Ryklin's hands at any moment.

I should have been safe in my own quarters, but it was the most dangerous place for me on Nebula Outpost. And I couldn't give anyone an indication that it worried me.

There was another possibility brewing deep inside of me. I'd let them take my soul to circumvent the Denya Price. What did it mean that my emotions were waking up after so many years of dormancy? If they came back fully, would I drop dead, the price finally catching up to me?

It might be kinder to my brethren if that were to happen.

But if I had the slightest inkling of the possibility, then I needed to stay far away from Pippa. I didn't want to imagine her horror at witnessing my death.

Zyrus's tablet beeped with an incoming message, which he read and then stood. "A woman was assaulted on the fourth level. I've been called to clean up the hallway."

"An assault?" My mind immediately went to Pippa, as if there weren't thousands of other women on the station. But she was the one that mattered most.

"Yes, a young Oscavian woman. This report indicates that she's been taken to the infirmary and has fallen into a coma."

"That's a lot of information for an order to clean up the mess."

Zyrus paused for a moment before nodding in acknowledgement. "I'm tapped into the med system and security reports. And, before you ask, I've been scanning for information about Fran's murder. Security is still working their theory about illegal table destruction, and the scans haven't come back from the lab to confirm whether or not the victim truly was this Fran woman. I will let you know the moment they're onto anything relevant."

"Thank you."

Zyrus left. I expected someone else would come to sit with me before long. I wasn't sure where Ryklin was; he'd mentioned having errands to run, and only a few moments after he'd left, Zyrus had shown up. I suspected I'd be followed if I took off on my own, and annoyance nipped at the back of my mind. That was an emotion I could do without.

No. I didn't want to let any of them go. Even if this was only a small gift before my end, I wanted to soak it up.

And there was only one person I wanted to be with.

The comm on the wall blinked with an incoming message from Pippa's quarters. I wondered why she didn't send it straight to my communicator, but then I remembered I hadn't given her those contact details. It was something I'd have to remedy soon.

I think I've found something big. Come to Section X43-2. You need to see this. -Pip

I had to call up a map of the station to see where she

was talking about. It was overflow housing that wasn't currently being used due to maintenance issues. The perfect place for someone to make a lair. And a very dangerous place for Pippa to be lurking alone.

I took off without bothering to reply to the message. If she was there, there wasn't a moment to waste.

Getting to X43-2 brought me through parts of the station I'd never seen before, most of them maintenance hallways that were undoubtedly supposed to be off-limits. No one tried to stop me.

There was no sign to indicate when I passed from one module of the station to another, but when I got to Sector X, something felt different, empty. The place smelled dusty, and though I could hear the ever-present hum of the machines that kept the station operational, there was no whisper of life around me, no footsteps, no voices.

I opened my mouth to call out for Pippa, but choked back the words. If Pippa was here, Fran's killer could be here too. I wouldn't give away my position like that, nor hers.

I ventured deeper into Sector X, reading off the different hallway numbers and searching for Pippa or whatever had brought her here. I didn't find anything. And when I got to 43-2, she wasn't there, and I saw no signs that she had been.

Something wasn't right.

I pulled my comm out of my pocket, but before I could even try and send a message, I heard the squeak of a footstep on the ground, a shadow moved over my shoulder, and something heavy crashed against the back of my head.

16

PIPPA

THE PANIC ATTACK came out of nowhere.

One minute I was calmly headed towards Noelle's room to invite her to get dinner with me, the next I was doubled over and heaving, my heart threatening to explode as the certainty of death washed over me.

Drex.

I needed Drex.

Instinct had me running towards the lifts, still barely able to breathe with sweat pouring down my face. I had to look like an absolute wreck and I didn't give a single damn. Drex would fix this.

I crossed the ship and got to his quarters in half the time it usually took me. And when I got to his door, I banged on it, desperate to be let in.

No one answered.

Oh no, I knew this would happen.

The certainty came deep within me, knowledge that something was wrong, and I needed to help. I wasn't psychic or anything, and my intuition had never been better than average, but right now I *knew*.

I tried the handle on the door and cried out in relief when it slid open. Drex didn't seem the type to leave his quarters unlocked, but I didn't question the good luck.

He wasn't there. The quarters were tiny. There were four bunks hooked to the walls on either side of the walkway. A small shower room was off to the corner and their kitchen area didn't even have a sink. But I wasn't there to look around.

I needed to find Drex.

The comm screen on the wall was lit up, and I checked it. What I saw made my stomach roil.

I think I've found something big. Come to Section X43-2. You need to see this. -Pip

I hadn't sent that message. It came from my room account, but I hadn't been in my room since leaving for my shift in the morning. Someone had either hacked my account or broken into my quarters.

No time to worry about that.

I left Drex's quarters on a mission to find Section X43-2. We'd been doing some maintenance work on the air filtration system in there lately, but no one was supposed to be there outside of their shift. The station disabled the life support system every night to preserve air on the rest of the ship, and the doors would be sealing shut in less than half an hour.

It would take me almost that long to get there.

I ran, all the while trying to convince myself that all would be well. Even if the doors closed, I could use my maintenance override code to get in and find Drex. And it wasn't like they sucked out all the air. There'd still be enough ambient oxygen to survive the night. No, it was the cold that would be the biggest danger. But maybe Detyens were more resilient to cold than humans.

I ran even faster.

Twenty-two minutes later, I crossed into Sector X. There was no flashing light warning that the life support system would be powering down. There was no need with everyone out of the sector.

"Drex!" I called out, heading toward hallway 43-2. "Drex, where are you?" My heart beat so rapidly I thought I was going to faint, and my lungs heaved with the effort to suck in enough air. Running was not my favorite activity, and I'd just done more of it in the last hour than I had in the past year.

I heard a groan and saw a dark form on the floor. A leg. I rushed forward and saw a disturbing puddle of green liquid right next to his head. He clutched it and moaned in pain, and sound meant he wasn't dead.

Was his blood green?

If so, he needed medical attention ASAP.

I saw a medkit on the wall and tore it down, ripping into it until I could find a cold pack and a bandage. I sealed up the nasty cut on the back of his head and covered it in the cold pack. Drex seemed kind of out of it still, and we were running out of time. I couldn't carry him, but there was no way I was leaving him here.

My eyes fell on a pressure injector, and I didn't give myself time to hesitate before I plucked it out of the box and pressed it against his arm. The mix of healing formula and stimulant made his eyes go wide, and when he stared at me, they flashed to red and stayed that way for several seconds. His mouth formed a word I couldn't make out before he rolled over and vomited right into the small puddle of his own blood.

I grabbed the small bottle of water that was

meant to cleanse wounds out of the medkit and handed it to him. He took it and rinsed his mouth out.

"Trap," he said.

"For you," I agreed, heart still racing. Adrenaline was making my hands shake and my whole body feel a bit wobbly. "Come on, we have to get out of here." I didn't know how long it had been since I'd arrived, but we couldn't have much time left. "They turn off life support in here every night. We have to get out."

I held out a hand to help him to his feet, but before we could stand, the lights overhead went out, and in the distance, I heard the sector doors shut and seal.

We were locked in, and it was about to get very cold.

17
DREX

The shockwave of recognition sparked through me the moment my mind cleared from the blow to the back of my head. It felt like electricity sizzled n my veins. There she was, hovering over me, and it all suddenly made sense.

My instinct was to reach up and grab her, to keep her close and never let her go. But someone had lured me to an empty part of the station and bashed my head in; there was no time for an embrace. I had to protect my mate. We had to get to safety.

At least I was on my feet by the time the lights went out, my hand clutched in my mate's. It was a perfect fit, a feeling I wanted to savor. But not just yet.

"Is there any way out?" I asked. My voice was raspy, as if I'd been unconscious for hours instead of minutes.

Her fingers squeezed mine, and I squeezed right back. "I know the maintenance override code to open the door. We just need to find it. I can't see a thing." Pippa's voice had a note of panic.

"Check the med kit; there may be a flashlight." Whatever she'd injected me with was making my heart race, but it had caused the pain to flee, and I'd take it. I wasn't even dizzy.

Pippa tugged on my hand and knelt, feeling around for the kit. I could hear a few items being moved around until she finally made a sound of triumph. "Got it!" She hit the switch, and a tiny shaft of light cut through the darkness. "Well, it's better than nothing. Come on, I know the way back."

We walked hand in hand through the dark sector, the air around us getting colder with every step. Pippa shivered, and I tugged her closer and draped my arm around her. If I had a jacket, I would have offered it. "Why shut down life support?" I asked.

She sighed. "No one lives out here yet, so they only keep it on when people are working in this sector, otherwise the whole area is sealed off."

That decision sounded liable to get someone killed. "There wasn't any warning about the lights; seems like anyone could sneak in here and get trapped." Kids on the station loved to explore, I was sure, or people needing an escape from their own quarters. Sector X had to be tempting.

Pippa made a humming sound. "Usually, the doors to the sector are locked, even when it's not sealed. It's weird that they were open."

Whoever laid the trap laid it well.

We finally made it to the air lock separating us from the rest of the station, and Pippa knelt down to examine the panel. She pressed her fingers against it, but nothing happened. "Hmm ..."

"What?"

She didn't respond. Instead, she yanked hard on the panel until it came off the wall, and then she examined the wires. "Damn it!"

"What is it?" It didn't sound good.

She took a deep breath. "Someone cut out the wires. No, they didn't just cut them, they removed any wires I could use to reset the machine to open the door. There's no way to open this door from this side." She slid fully to the ground and thumped her head back against the door.

I sat down beside her, and she leaned in close. She shut off the light so there was nothing but darkness to keep us company. "There's no other door to the sector?"

"Not unless you want to take a space walk."

"That would not be ideal." My skin prickled in the cold. We had to be approaching freezing. "How cold will it get?"

"It shouldn't be much worse than this as long as the insulation holds up. We won't run out of air." She took a deep breath as if to demonstrate her confidence.

"Do you have your comm?" I'd checked my pocket, but mine was gone, no doubt taken by whoever had attacked me.

Pippa shifted and pulled it out. The screen lit up, almost blinding me in the darkness. Then a warning popped up. "You have to be fucking kidding me! No signal? We're on the freaking station."

"It wouldn't take much to jam it," I said. "Or perhaps there's equipment here interfering with your comm."

She snorted in disbelief.

Fair enough, I didn't believe that either.

"We should find something warm to wear and a place to make camp for the night. I promise you, I've survived worse." The Detyen Legion's home base was on an icy moon inhospitable to most life. Part of training had involved surviving for a week on the tundra with few supplies. This was nothing.

"You sound different," Pippa said. "That blow to the head didn't do something to you, did it?"

It wasn't the time to tell her who she was to me, not while we were trapped together on this part of the station. But I couldn't stop myself from leaning in and kissing her, just long enough to savor the taste of her lips. "I'm fine. Let's go."

She hesitated for a moment, as if she wanted to say something, but then stood, and we started moving.

Navigating by pen light wasn't easy, but my eyes began to adjust after awhile. We passed by an escape pod, and I held up a hand to stop her. There was a survival pack on the wall beside the exit. "Can we navigate the pod to somewhere on the rest of the station?" I asked.

She gave a sad shake of her head. "Maybe if there was a pod there, but they haven't been installed yet. If you hit the escape button now, you'll just get sucked into space."

"Not ideal."

"No," she agreed.

At least the survival pack was full. I pulled out the first insulated space suit and handed it over to Pippa. There was a second that I took for myself. We didn't plan to space walk, but the suits would keep us warmer through the night. Even better, each of the suits had a hefty light attached so we could see our surroundings much better. No more navigating by pen light.

And, finally, there were air canisters built into each suit. They made them heavy, but if the air got low, we could seal our helmets, and each of us would have a couple of hours for help to find us.

A loud creaking noise echoed throughout the hallway, and it made me pause. "What was that?"

"I don't know. Probably just normal space station sounds." Pippa didn't seem concerned.

There was a loud crack, and the floor under us shuddered. Pippa stumbled towards me, and then we were both falling up as gravity gave way.

Pippa clung to me, and I held on just as tightly. But we were floating free in the hall, and we needed an anchor. I reached out and grabbed onto the wall, pulling a clip from the side of my spacesuit and securing it to keep us from falling any farther. "Does life support control the gravity drive?" I asked. If so, it should have been cut the moment we were locked in.

"No." Pippa's eyes were wide, panic suffusing her face. She'd been handling it well, but now she looked on the verge of hyperventilating. "I think the sector's been jettisoned."

I suddenly longed for those cold nights at Detyen HQ.

But there was no time to ponder. If we'd been jettisoned, we'd fall away fast from Nebula Outpost and get burned up in the atmosphere of Nebula. But our space suits were already on. "Seal your helmet," I told my mate.

Pippa's eyes widened even farther, but she took a deep breath and did as I instructed. I sealed my own helmet and was thankful when the visor screen lit up.

"Can you hear me?" I asked.

"Yes," her voice crackled over the built in radio. Whatever was jamming her comm signal wasn't affecting this communication. Good.

I unhooked myself from the wall and anchored the hook to Pippa's belt. "We have to go out the escape hatch," I told her. "There are thrusters in these suits. We can make it to the station as long as we're close." I didn't mention that if we'd fallen too far already, we'd end up floating in space until our air ran out. No reason to dwell.

"Do it." Pippa's voice was firm.

I pulled us down and pressed the escape button, hoping whoever had sabotaged the main door hadn't thought to wreck this as well. My doubt barely had time to form before the door slid open and we were sucked out into the vacuum of space.

It was eerily silent after the creaking and groaning of the station.

"Fire your thrusters in one, two, three." We fired at the same time and launched away from the falling sector. Nebula Outpost was a behemoth from the outside. I hadn't been off of the station since I first landed, and it was easy to ignore just how massive the place was.

Now, staring at the dark side, I was struck by its beauty. I could make out the blinking lights of airlocks and the vast expanse of solar panels catching energy for the entire station.

But the beauty would pulverize us if we didn't get our approach right.

We hadn't fallen far, not yet. I didn't look back to see what Sector X looked like as it hurtled toward Nebula. Newly awakened emotions were churning in me, and there was no telling what I'd do if I was suddenly hit by a burst of panic. I had to be strong now for my mate and for my life.

I'd just found her, I refused to lose her now.

Pippa pointed to a small hatch that was barely visible on the side of the station, and we navigated towards it with careful bursts of thrust. It felt like climbing a mountain, but even more treacherous as there was nothing to hold onto and no way to guide ourselves except the thrust in our boots and gloves.

We hit the side of the station, and Pippa used one of her hooks to anchor outside the door. She pressed a large yellow button, and a small hatch opened, allowing us to enter an airlock. Pippa unclipped her hook, and we entered. She pressed another button and the door closed and we crashed to the floor, suddenly caught in the station's gravity.

I unsealed my helmet, and she threw herself at me, wrapping me tight in her arms. I held on and soaked up the contact. It didn't hurt anymore. Nothing did, not now that we were safe.

18

PIPPA

WE DIDN'T STICK AROUND to see if anyone was monitoring the air lock. Given the incompetence of station security, I feared they might accuse us of purposefully sneaking onto Sector X and jettisoning it from the station. Drex agreed that waiting around would be a waste of time.

I didn't need to ask him to come back to my room with me. He simply took my hand and walked with me. I couldn't be alone right now. I couldn't be away from him. I would remember what he looked like lying there with all that blood around him for the rest of my life, and I never wanted to see something like that again.

He needed to be okay. And I needed to see that.

There were a dozen things we needed to talk

about. Someone had tried to kill us, and they knew enough about the station to jettison an entire sector. That had to be a clue.

But my brain was moving at a million kilometers a second, and I couldn't concentrate enough to put pieces together.

Then we got inside my room, and everything stilled until I could only focus on one thing. We were both alive. And that was all that mattered.

Drex looked down at me and his eyes flared red and then we were on each other, lips crashing together in a desperate kiss. I needed to feel his warmth, the life coursing through him. He gripped me tightly and held me so close I didn't know where I ended and he began.

He groaned into my mouth, and I took him in, tongue dancing with his as I lost myself in the moment. My hands flew up, and I clutched at him, as if letting go meant losing him forever. If I let go, I might remember what it felt like to be surrounded by the nothingness of space, one wrong move away from certain death.

Space was a free fall, but it felt nothing like this.

Drex pulled away, breathing heavily and still holding me tight. I felt something wet against my cheeks and realized I was crying. He brushed his thumb over my cheek and kissed my forehead. "You're safe with me," he vowed. "Always."

As if I had any doubt. I leaned in and kissed him again, gentler this time, but no less passionate. I was safe, but that didn't mean I didn't need him.

His lips trailed down my neck, and I sighed in pleasure, sinking into his touch. I wasn't thinking about anything else, just this moment, the two of us and the feelings thrumming between us.

I remembered everything he'd told me the other night, about what it meant to be soulless and how his emotions just weren't there anymore. But I couldn't believe it, not here, not now.

Explanations could wait for later.

His shirt was rough against my fingers, and I needed skin. Needed to feel him. My hands slipped underneath the hem and found the warmth of his flesh. He pulled back and ripped the shirt over his head. His eyes were still glowing red, everything about him so intense it threatened to overpower me in the best way possible. My whole body was strung tight with desire for this man.

Our mouths crashed together again, and he wrapped his arms around me and lifted me up, carrying me towards my bed. As he set me down, I wriggled out of my own shirt and cast it aside. I didn't want there to be any doubt about what I wanted tonight. I had Drex in my bed. We were both alive.

We needed this.

My pants went next, my underwear going with them, and I laid back on the mattress, completely naked. The look in Drex's eyes nearly set me on fire. His nostrils flared, and he came down on me, holding himself over me as he took a kiss that stole the air from my lungs. His hand traveled down my side, setting my skin alight with the touch of his callused palm.

He cupped my breast, his fingers finding my nipple and rolling it until I moaned into his mouth. It felt like pure electricity arcing between the two of us. I never wanted it to stop.

Drex continued his exploration, sliding his fingers farther south until he reached the apex of my thighs and then lower. He teased at my opening, tracing it lightly with the pads of his fingers, making me arch in need.

He growled, a deep, guttural sound, and suddenly the teasing was done. His fingers dipped inside of me, and he captured my cry of pleasure with a kiss.

I bucked my hips as he touched me, building me

higher and higher until all I could do was moan. My legs shook, and my hands clutched at his shoulders, afraid to fall into the abyss without him. I felt so empty, and I needed something inside me, but Drex's merciless fingers drew me over the edge until I was flying, my body rippling around him.

His pants disappeared somewhere in the haze of pleasure, and with my body still singing from the joy of release, I felt the blunt head of his cock tease my entrance. "Are you ready?" he asked me.

"Yes." The word came out in a husky whisper. I needed this, him, everything.

He pushed into me slowly, every inch lighting up every nerve ending in my body. I cried out, my nails digging into his shoulder blades. He was so big, and I was so full, I didn't think I could take any more. But then he seated fully, and I rocked my hips against him, adjusting to his size and wanting more.

With a groan, he pulled almost entirely out and then slammed back in. Pleasure flooded my system as he rocked back and forth, driving me mad with every stroke. I held onto him, clinging to this moment with everything I had as the waves of sensation carried me to a different world.

Drex's movements sped up, his thrusts growing faster and deeper. Our bodies tangled together, and sweat dripped off of him. I didn't know where he ended and where I started. All that mattered was this joining.

Drex bit down on my shoulder and roared, his cum pumping into me and sending me careening over the edge into bliss once more.

I felt the strangest sensation of something snapping into place, a bond I didn't know but needed more than breath. It reached out from somewhere right below my heart and connected me to Drex in a way that I already knew could never be broken. I clutched his shoulder, chest heaving in exertion, but before I could say anything, his eyes flared the brightest red I'd ever seen, then they rolled into the back of his head, and he went limp.

19
DREX

EVERYTHING WAS bright when I opened my eyes. Bright and loud.

And my denya was right there, eyes wide and worried as she looked down at me. "You passed out," she said.

I could feel the bond deep in my chest, a cord anchoring me to her. "You're here," was all I could respond. Nothing felt quite real, but everything *felt*. I wasn't sure how I'd survived for the last seven years without this.

"Of course I'm here, like I'd leave you." Her worry was starting to slide into exasperation.

I pulled her close and kissed her. Whatever echoes of pain I'd felt were gone, the vestiges of my reawakening soul fully healed by the bond with my mate. I didn't understand how this was possible; I'd never heard a word of it. But this was no mistake.

She was mine.

The second time fried my brain just as much as the first, but there was no passing out, and as we fell asleep tangled up with one another, I knew I'd do anything to make sure I had this every night of my future.

All the rest of our problems were waiting for us the moment we woke up.

Pippa made two cups of coffee and ordered a small breakfast from her food machine while I washed up in her shower. We sat beside each other, and every time she smiled at me, I could feel my lips pull up in the unfamiliar motion. It had been years since I felt the urge to smile, now I never wanted to stop.

"I know someone tried to kill us, but we need to talk about this first," she said, waving her fork at me. "Because the last time we talked, you told me you didn't feel anything. And I don't think someone incapable of emotion could have sex like that."

We were eating some kind of sweet toast battered in eggs, and it made my taste buds dance. I'd survived on nutrient drinks and meal replacement bars ever since the procedure. Flavorful foods were seen as too stimulating. And the few times I'd eaten regular food, it had been little better than grit.

"You're my denya." It was a guiding beacon of truth for me, and because of it, everything made sense.

She dropped the fork and narrowed her eyes in suspicion. "You said that word before."

I reached for her hand and held it tight. "You're my mate. Last night sealed the bond between us."

Her eyes widened, and she gulped. "That seems like a major step. When did you plan on mentioning that to me?"

There were things I could tell her to ease her fear. Often if Detyens recognized a mating bond they'd seal it as quickly as possible, just in case they were parted again. It wasn't inherently romantic, just a twist of biology and fate. But I didn't understand how a person could walk away.

"I didn't realize it; I didn't think it was possible. When we give up our souls, we sacrifice any hope for the future. There isn't supposed to be a mate for us, no feelings, nothing. But it's back, all of it." And with it came the delayed panic from our impromptu space walk last night. "Someone tried to kill us."

"We're still on this mating talk." She didn't let go

of my hand, but her voice was firm. "Don't change the subject."

Perhaps it wasn't appropriate, but that startled a laugh out of me. It was short, more like a cough, and I cut myself off, too surprised to keep going.

"You kind of look like a dog surprised by its own bark." She bit her lip, but the smile was still there.

"I haven't laughed in seven years."

Her expression turned grave. "That's a hell of a thing." She pulled her hand away. "We barely know each other. How can we …"

"I'm not asking for everything." Yet. If she gave the word, I'd never leave her side. Need pulsed through me, and it was more then sexual. I wanted her. I liked her. She was a gift from fate. "I could not hide this from you even if I wished to. Can't you feel the bond?" I placed a hand on my chest.

She mirrored the movement, and her chin dipped slightly, almost absently, like she wasn't doing it on purpose. "I feel it."

"We can continue as we have, find our own way together at our own pace. We know the bond is there, but it doesn't control us." Nothing in me wanted to slow down, but I'd give my denya what she needed.

She didn't respond for several moments. Then, "Someone tried to kill us last night."

So, now it was time to change the subject. I didn't argue. We needed to get to the bottom of this before anyone else got hurt. Which reminded me of what Zyrus had said. "Another woman was attacked."

Pippa gasped and covered her mouth. "Oh, no."

"She survived, and she's in a coma, or she was as of last night. It could be unconnected, but Zyrus wouldn't have told me something irrelevant."

"Who's Zyrus?"

"Another one of the Detyens who has ended up here. He's a tech specialist and is assisting Ryklin and I in the investigation." It still troubled me to speak of my brethren, even with my denya. More than half a decade of secrecy did not break easily, though I had no doubt I could trust her.

"How many of you are there?" she asked. "On the station, I mean, not looking into the murder."

"Six of us. I've been here the longest, followed by Ryklin. Thalor's only been with us about six months. We're all—*they're* all soulless." It was strange to consider that I no longer was. I had my soul back, my emotions. And I wasn't sure how to share that with them or if I should at all. It couldn't happen;

Ryklin might think this was another step toward fixation.

I'd forgotten worry, and it was not welcome back.

"What is it?" Pippa asked.

"I'll have to handle this news carefully. I've never heard of a soulless Detyen finding his mate before, and neither have the others." I couldn't lie to her.

She nodded and didn't press. "Whoever contacted you last night had to know the inner workings of the ship pretty well," she said. "It's not exactly easy to jettison an entire sector. For any of the populated sectors, you'd need codes from the ruling council, though there may be an emergency override in case of catastrophic failure or fire. But not just anyone would know that."

"You think Sector X was different?" I was glad we'd been the only two people there, though I'd much rather my mate was always far from danger.

"I do." She thought about it for a moment. "I've worked in that sector, and it's the only newly constructed sector I have experience with. I'm trying to remember the safety brief, but those kinds of things blur, you know. I think the maintenance supervisors gave jettison codes to a few team leaders, just in case there was an emergency. And the construction crew would have definitely had them. Since the sector wasn't fully operational yet, it's possible that those codes were still programmed into the system."

"You think it was someone in maintenance." It made sense. A regular person on the station wouldn't know how to operate the incinerators or that the life support was turned off in Sector X every night.

Her lip quivered, and she squeezed her eyes shut. "I don't want it to be. I know all the maintenance crew, mostly. None of them seem like murderers. What if it really was just a table leg in the incinerator? What if Fran's off visiting relatives and didn't tell anyone? Maybe there was a mechanical failure that lead to ..." She pushed up from the table and started to pace.

I touched the back of my head. It was a little tender, but the healing serum Pippa had given me had done its job well. "Someone lured me there. Someone knocked me out. Someone attacked that woman." I understood why she didn't want to consider her colleagues might be killers, but this was no accident.

"I should have never started to look into this."

I was out of my seat in a heartbeat and gathered

her in my arms. She wasn't backing down from the investigation, I knew that, and I wasn't stupid enough to suggest it. "We'll figure this out," I promised.

And we had to do it soon. The next time someone tried to kill us, we might not be so lucky.

20

DREX

"We need a record of everyone who has authorization to jettison portions of the ship," I said as I returned to my quarters, my face a careful mask of neutrality.

Pippa had to return for her shift. No one knew about our daring space walk the night before, and we'd both decided that keeping it quiet was for the best. We didn't want the murderer to know how close he'd come to stopping us. And if station security learned of our presence, they might start to investigate us. No need for complications.

"Where were you last night?" Ryklin asked. He was finishing up his own breakfast and cleaned the table.

News of the jettisoned sector was already

starting to whisper its way through the halls of Nebula Outpost, and undoubtedly Ryklin had heard something by now. "I stayed with Pippa. We were lured to Sector X and had to escape once it was jettisoned." It was difficult to keep to the facts, to keep my expression from betraying anything. This couldn't last for long; of that I was certain. Something would betray me to one of my men.

What would they do then? How could I explain that this wasn't fixation, wasn't some kind of flaw? Hopefully it would wait until after we were done with this investigation. I could feel that we were getting close, though my instincts were rusty from disuse. Did conviction always feel like that?

"I thought you decided to stay away from that human." There couldn't be any judgement in Ryklin's voice; he wasn't capable. I felt it all the same.

"I changed my mind." And I couldn't let him question me more. I'd give something away. "Have you read the messages on the comm?" I asked, nodding towards the unit on the wall.

"There are no messages."

What? I crossed to the screen and woke it up and saw that Ryklin was right. If Ryklin weren't right beside me, I might have cursed. "Last night, I received a message from Pippa's room account that she had discovered something in Sector X and needed me to join her. When I did, someone attacked me from behind and knocked me out. I must have accidentally left the door to our quarters unlocked because Pippa came here, found the message, and then found me. She administered first aid, and then life support was shut off to the sector, which she informs me is standard practice, and the sector was jettisoned. We exited via an escape hatch, and were able to navigate to another airlock on the ship." It was a dispassionate account of the most important night of my life, and I was frayed at the edges trying to keep my face from betraying anything I felt to a man I'd known for years.

Ryklin stared at me, his expression the closest to shock I'd ever seen on a soulless face. "That is … What?"

His surprise had a strange steadying effect. Perhaps not even the most soulless of creatures could remain completely unbothered by last night. "I suspect that whoever is behind the attacks attempted to murder me last night." Pippa seemed to think the killer was after us both, but I was the only one who'd been lured out. If I hadn't left the room unlocked, she never would have found me in time.

I had never quite believed in fate before, but it was the only explanation I had for last night.

Maybe if I explained it correctly, Ryklin would understand. But I couldn't risk it yet.

"I'm certain Zyrus can find that information." He paused for a moment. "It seems that your presence may endanger the human. I would suggest you minimize it."

It was logical. If the killer had focused on me, she could be caught in the crossfire. But we'd only just bonded, and I couldn't leave her alone. I needed to be near her to keep her safe. Neither of us would have survived Sector X alone.

"She is dedicated to this investigation. If someone isn't there to watch her back, she'll be just as vulnerable." It sounded logical, and I didn't owe any explanation to Ryklin, but his agreement would make this easier.

He shrugged. "You may be making yourselves into bait. Perhaps that will make this attacker easier to find."

It wasn't my plan, but I didn't respond. I needed this investigation to be over.

I wanted life with my mate.

21

PIPPA

Denya. Mate. Drex. Words kept echoing around in my head, and even though things on the station were beyond scary, I couldn't stop smiling.

I had a mate. How cool was that?

It wasn't something I'd ever imagined before. Humans didn't really do that, but I'd grown up among all the aliens on Nebula Outpost and knew that for some of them, a mating bond was closer than anything I could imagine. Some could even speak mind to mind.

Drex? I tried to project the thought out of my brain, but all that did was make my eye twitch, and I didn't receive an answer.

Though the prospect of mind-to-mind speech sounded cool right now, I'd probably be thankful my mate couldn't read my mind once I learned he didn't pick up his dirty towels or that he made strange mouth noises when he ate.

Even that made me smile.

I wanted to talk to Noelle about it. Hell, I wanted to tell the world. But my best friend was a good first step. Unfortunately, she was working on a distant part of the space station, and I wouldn't see her for hours.

Maybe I could say something to Darian. After all, he was Detyen, he'd understand.

But the thought barely crossed my mind before I dismissed it. As far as I knew, Darian didn't have a denya, which meant he was staring down the end of a very short lifespan. Telling him about Drex and I might just be rubbing that in his face.

I finished up my work early and was out of the locker room before anyone else had filtered in from their assignments. Drex had his own work to finish up and wouldn't be dismissed from his shift for another hour or so.

Then I remembered what he told me about the woman who'd been attacked. No news had come out on the station bulletins, and I hadn't heard any whispers. I tried to remember if anyone had been absent from their shifts for the past few days, but no one came to mind.

Security was keeping it quiet. And even if they hadn't been, any news of her would be forgotten in the wake of the jettisoning of Sector X. The only news on *that* right now was that they were investigating. I'd heard half a dozen rumors already ranging from catastrophic mechanical failure that was going to doom the entire ship to drug runners using it as a distraction to launch ships from a secret colony on Nebula. I'd kept my mouth shut through all the whispers.

Without really thinking about it, I let my feet take me towards the infirmary wing. I wanted to know if the woman—whoever she was—had woken up. Maybe she could tell someone what her attacker looked like. Maybe she even knew who they were.

When I closed my eyes, I still saw the shadow of my attacker moving in the dark, and part of me wanted to see what might have happened if I hadn't managed to get away.

It made me a terrible person, selfish and gawking at another woman's pain. But it wasn't like I planned to tell her that, so I hoped that made it all right.

Somehow, I doubted it.

The infirmary wing was as busy and bustling as always. I hadn't spent much time here since I broke my arm after a nasty fall while repairing a vent where I lost my footing on the ladder and plunged to the ground. I'd been diligent about safety harnesses and hooks ever since.

The bustle made it easy to slip in unnoticed. Only the sickest of patients were kept for longer than overnight here, otherwise they were sent back to their rooms with a portable medbot to monitor them if necessary and strict instructions to call if anything went amiss.

I found the corridor that led to the long-term patient ward and walked like I knew where I was going. One of the rooms held an old man on a breathing machine, his skin withered to brittle paper and his eyes closed. The next room held a large tank filled with green liquid in which rested an alien I couldn't identify.

The third room held a human woman. A medbot with dozens of wires coming out of it hung on the wall, all those wires affixed to her. Her face was swollen and bruised, and half of it was covered by a bandage. Her hands were also bandaged, and one of her legs was in a cast.

She didn't look like she'd be waking up anytime soon.

I heard footsteps coming down the hallway and moved on before I was caught snooping. No one else was in the long-term ward, which meant the woman was the victim.

That could have been me.

Bile rose in my throat, and I had to swallow it down. The last place I wanted to get sick was the infirmary ward. I didn't need some medbot fussing over me.

Once I was outside of the infirmary, I was able to breathe fully. I wasn't the woman in the long-term ward. I'd escaped. Twice. I was safe.

Or as safe as I could be with a killer on the loose.

There was the bile again.

"Pippa? Are you alright?" I felt a hand on my back and looked up to see Darian standing over me, a concerned expression written plainly across his face. "Are you sick?"

I straightened and forced a smile. Then I shifted just enough so his hand fell off my back. His touch felt too heavy, more like he was holding me down instead of offering support. "I'm fine," I assured him. "What are you doing here?"

"I could ask the same of you." His eyes flicked up and down. "Did you injure yourself?"

I would have told Noelle why I was there. I was definitely planning to tell Drex. But I couldn't make my mouth explain it to Darian, and I wasn't sure why. He couldn't be happy with the fact that we had a murderer roaming the ship, attacking random women. Then again, he hadn't said much about it to me.

"I'm fine," I repeated. "I'm just taking a walk. What about you?"

His concerned expression faded, and for just a second, his face was completely blank before it shifted into his standard smile. "I just needed to pick up some healing balm. My palms have been cracking like crazy." He held up his hands, but they looked normal and unblemished to me.

He pointed to the vending machine beside the door. It was stocked with medical supplies and accessible to anyone on the ship.

"Oh. Um, the green one really helps me when my skin gets dry," I said. The balms came in different colors, both to indicate different strengths and formulations.

"Good tip." He studied the offerings and made his selection—green, like I suggested. "You hungry?"

he asked. "There's a restaurant at this end of the station I've been meaning to try."

Darian was my friend. I'd known him for years. He loved eating out with people, and I'd done it a ton of times before. I hadn't had a meal with him since this whole thing with the murders and Drex and mating started. I owed him one, I'd even promised him. But something made me hold back.

"Not tonight," I said. "I've gotta get back to my quarters. I'll see you later." I walked away before he could try and convince me otherwise.

Was this part of the whole denya thing? Was I being weird about spending time with another man because I was Drex's mate? I sure as hell hoped not. I had male friends, it was normal. And just because I was in love with—

Holy shit, was I in love with Drex?

It derailed my thoughts about Darian, that was for sure.

I couldn't be in love with him so soon, could I? How long had we known each other? A week? A little more than that?

I didn't fall fast, and I certainly didn't fall hard. I'd casually dated a few guys, but no one had ever made me yearn the way Drex did.

I was his mate. Fate had put its finger on the

scale and decided we were meant for one another before we even met. I'd literally made him feel emotion after nearly a decade of emptiness.

Was I supposed to tell him right now? The realization of my feelings made me a bit unsteady on my feet, and I wasn't sure of the process here. I'd never told a lover I loved them before.

My job had manuals. Every machine, every fix, it was written down somewhere. Even the little idiosyncrasies and tricks that were unique to each specific machine eventually made it to someone's notes. If I ever had a doubt about what I was supposed to do, I could look it up.

I didn't think there was a manual for falling in love. I'd certainly never heard of one.

And falling in love with a man who'd forgotten how to smile for seven years? Yeah, there definitely wasn't a manual for that.

I passed from one corridor into a high-ceilinged atrium. The center was filled with thick-leafed trees surrounded by lush green plants that made the whole area smell fresh and almost like we were down on some planet somewhere. Or, at least I assumed that's what it smelled like. The only planet I'd ever set foot on was Nebula, and that was when I was a small child and my parents had been able to afford a weekend at the small resort that used to be there. I didn't remember it.

I smiled at the plants. They reminded me of Drex. It was his job to keep them alive, and that couldn't be easy on a space station where the sunlight blasted through with too much radiation and heat with no natural atmosphere to protect us. The station had shields, but I had an idea that plants were more finicky than people.

A tall, blue figure was tending to some of the bushes at the far end of the atrium, and I smiled for a moment before I realized the tall blue figure wasn't my mate; it was Ryklin.

Could I get away without him seeing me? Maybe, if I hadn't stopped to enjoy the trees. Unfortunately, he looked up before I could walk away.

His face was just as blank as Drex's was when I first met him. I knew he couldn't have any negative feelings for me. He didn't have any at all. It must have been my imagination when I thought his eyes narrowed.

He stood up and put his tools aside, wiping a bit of dirt from his hands onto his overalls. "Pippa, please wait," he called, making it very clear he'd seen me.

I was being weird. First with Darian, now him.

Maybe this was some strange side effect of the mating bond. And since I had no intention of letting it curtail my friendships out of some weird fate-based jealousy, I forced myself to approach Ryklin. He was Drex's friend, sort of, as much as they could be friends given their condition.

"Hello, Ryklin." He didn't know that I knew what he was. Why would I ever assume it? His expression was neutral, but if I hadn't known he was soulless, I might have called it guarded. I was his friend's new girlfriend; it wasn't out of place.

But he couldn't care about Drex, so why did I get the impression he was about to warn me off?

"We aren't near your quarters," he observed.

Everyone just had to point that out. Ryklin was helping Drex and I investigate the murder, and he knew about the woman in the infirmary. Telling him why I was here shouldn't hurt anything. But I didn't. "I'm taking a walk."

"Have you seen Drex lately?" he asked.

"Not since this morning." He'd stayed the whole night. I'd thought my bed might be too small for two, but when we cuddled that close, space wasn't an issue. I hoped with all my heart he planned to come back tonight. "Why? Are you looking for him?"

"No, he came back to our quarters before work."

He was quiet for a moment, and I didn't fill the silence. "Drex is a danger to you. You need to pack a bag and take the first shuttle off this station. Take that friend of yours for good measure, Noelle. There's no time to waste."

"How do you know Noelle?" He might have seen her when he came to my room after the attack, but I didn't know they'd been introduced.

Ryklin dismissed my question. "Irrelevant." He reached into his pocket and pulled out a dark, slim cylinder. Credits. They were mostly digital, but credit cylinders were useful when we were far away from any data connection and needed to transfer funds. "Take this and leave Nebula Outpost."

I was tempted to take the credits just to teach him a lesson. Then I'd treat Drex and myself to something nice. Instead, I glared. I wasn't taking his money. "Drex wouldn't hurt me. Ever. And he certainly won't hurt Noelle. He doesn't even ... Never mind. I don't know what game you're trying to play, but stop. I'm not leaving this ship, or Drex."

"There are things you don't understand about him, about his past," Ryklin insisted.

He didn't know what Drex had told me. He couldn't know that I knew everything. And I certainly wasn't about to tell him.

"Mind your own business, Ryklin. Stay out of mine." I turned on my heel and stormed out of the atrium.

Drex had told me that he'd have to handle his brethren carefully, that they wouldn't understand what was going on between us, and Ryklin had just proven it. He wanted to separate me and Drex.

Why would he think Drex was a danger to me?

The question echoed in my head as I made my way back to my room. Why would Ryklin want me off the ship? He said he cared for my safety, but only in relation to Drex. And what did Noelle have to do with anything? I don't think she and Drex had exchanged more than a few pleasantries, if they'd ever talked at all.

Ryklin knew the trick to getting into locked rooms.

The realization hit me like a falling wrench, and I actually stumbled and had to catch myself against the wall.

The landscaping crews had also been working in the atrium in Sector X. He'd know about the life support.

I had no reason to think he knew how to jettison part of the station, but maybe he could.

Did he want me off the ship because I was too

close to Drex? Or because Drex and I were getting too close to the truth?

But, no. Not possible. Ryklin was soulless, just like Drex had been. He didn't feel anything. Why would he want to kill?

He had no motive.

And I was pretty sure he couldn't have attacked me. He'd been at my doorway before I made it back. He couldn't have done that unless there was some hidden passage that even I didn't know about. And maintenance knew about every passage and shortcut on the ship.

I didn't know why Ryklin would do it, but now the suspicion was lodged in my head, and it troubled me all the way back to my room.

22

PIPPA

DREX WAS WAITING outside my door when I made it to my room, and the smile that lit up his face made my heart sing. Whatever emotion the denya bond was working, it was bringing him fully back into this world, and I wanted to help him rediscover everything he'd forgotten.

But my thoughts of Ryklin still troubled me.

My mate moved aside to let me open the door, and the moment we were inside my quarters, his hands went to my waist, his lips on my neck as he kissed me from behind. "I spent all day imagining this," he whispered against me.

I leaned back into him, troubled thoughts dissolving under his touch.

"Tell me more." I arched my neck to give him better access, my skin prickling in delight.

His teeth nipped the sensitive spot where my shoulder met my neck, and his breath was hot on my ear. "I pictured you naked, waiting for me in your bed so that I could kiss every part of you until you begged for me to take you."

"Not bad at all." His fingers dipped under my shirt and found sensitive skin. I shivered and pressed my hips against him, already wanting more. "What else did you picture?"

He pulled away and took my hand, leading me towards my bed. "You, naked and spread out before me like a goddess, writhing on my tongue and moaning my name. And then me, buried deep inside of you, feeling you clench around me as you screamed."

Heat sizzled through me, and my whole body was tight with need. "How long were you holding that in?"

"It was a long shift." He pulled my shirt off and tossed it on the floor. "I need to taste you." His eyes flared red, and he guided me back to the bed and came right with me, lips finding my breast.

I cried out as he drew my nipple into his mouth, suckling it, his teeth scraping over delicate skin and sending a zing of sensation right between my legs. "Oh, fuck."

His eyes flashed again, and he kept it up until my nipple was hard, my whole body hot with need for him. He had a single-minded focus that blew my mind, like he forgot everything else in the galaxy except for touching and tasting me.

He moved to my other breast, and his fingers found the snap of my pants, working them open and pushing them down over my hips. If he wanted me fully naked, he'd have to stop playing with my breasts, and from the way he growled as I tried to shimmy my pants off, he didn't want that.

Oh, poor me. I just had to lay there and be a gorgeous alien's plaything.

And then he slipped his fingers between my legs, and I moaned.

"You're already so wet for me," he groaned against my skin. "So ready." He stroked me, his fingers circling over my swollen sex. "You're perfect."

I wanted to respond, but it was all I could do to concentrate on breathing as the pleasure built within me, pushing me higher and higher, the wave threatening to crash over me.

Drex was still fully clothed. That didn't seem

fair. I grabbed at his shirt, pulling it up over his head. He paused for just a moment to get it off, and then he was back, his face buried against my chest, his fingers stroking me closer and closer.

"Drex, please," I begged, so close. "I need you."

"I've got you," he murmured. He kissed his way down my body, spreading my legs wide. He gave me a wicked grin, his mouth mere inches from where I wanted him.

This was torture. Beautiful, beautiful torture.

And I never wanted it to end.

He started with light kisses against my inner thighs, teasing me. I moaned and bucked my hips, wanting more. But he held me still with one arm, keeping me exactly where he wanted me.

His tongue circled my sex, his fingers still massaging my entrance. My whole body was one quivering nerve ending, primed for pleasure and so close I was nearly crying with need.

And then he sucked on my clit, and stars exploded behind my eyes.

But before the orgasm could take me, Drex pulled back, gentling his touches just enough so that I didn't tumble over the edge.

I gasped something out, it might have been a word, but all I could think about was him, what he was doing to me. I buried my fingers in his hair, tugging on it, encouraging him.

And then he did it again, his fingers teasing me, his tongue working magic until I couldn't stand it anymore.

I felt more, too much, not enough. I didn't know it was possible to feel this much pleasure and not explode from it.

And then he shifted just a little, and my vision went white.

Every part of my body shook with pleasure, from the tips of my toes to my very soul. I couldn't remember ever coming so hard in my life. I don't think I remembered my own name.

When I finally came back to earth, Drex was over me, his clothes gone and his eyes red. He positioned himself between my thighs and kissed me softly, his hand cupping my chin.

"Forever, denya," he swore.

I stared up at him, remembering how scared I'd been to love him only a few hours ago. Here, I knew I couldn't have any doubt. Here, I knew I'd never stood a chance.

He eased his way into me slowly, giving me a moment to adjust to him. When I wrapped my arms around his shoulders and dug my fingers into his back, he moaned my name and thrust home.

My body should have been spent, the pleasure from his tongue more than enough to last the night, but already I was heating up again. I loved the feel of him inside me, so big and powerful. He shifted so he could caress my breasts again, and I shuddered, too lost in him to form words.

His gaze was possessive, his touches reverent, as if he couldn't believe that he'd found me. He kissed me again and rocked his hips forward, giving me just enough friction to make me gasp.

I let myself get lost in the moment. Let myself drown in the sensations building within me and lose myself in my mate. This was everything I hadn't known I'd always needed, everything I never wanted to give up.

His pace quickened as he fucked me harder, deeper, until I thought we might both go mad with need. But we were already there, and there was only one way to satisfy it.

His body tensed, his face contorted with pleasure, and then he was coming, pumping me full, his cries mixing with mine and taking me over that edge with him.

We rode the wave together, our bodies entwined, until the last tremors died down.

We laid there together, letting our bodies cool, letting the heat die down, but we never stopped touching. "I'm going to make you strip for me soon," I warned him.

He played with a strand of my hair, and his eyebrows quirked up. "What? Why?"

I grabbed his hand and kissed his fingers. "You keep getting me naked, and I've barely seen you. Doesn't seem fair."

He rolled to the side and spread his hands wide. "Take your fill, denya."

The man was gorgeous, and he knew it. And he was all mine.

I just had to find a way to keep him forever.

23
DREX

IT WAS a shame the shower wasn't big enough for two. But perhaps for the best. If I stayed with my mate in the shower, we wouldn't do anything else. My stomach growled, letting me know that I was hungry, and I wanted to talk to her.

I wanted everything.

Want had come back in a roaring wave over the last day, an emotion that had seemed so ... petty ... and now consumed me like nothing else.

Pippa's hair was still damp when she joined me in the eating area, and I wrapped her in my arms and took the kiss I craved. She moaned against me, hands clutching my shoulders. When she pulled back, her pupils were blown wide, and she looked a bit dazed.

I liked putting that look on her face.

She blinked a few times and then shook her head to clear it. "What do you want for dinner?"

"I normally eat an unflavored protein and nutrient bowl." It provided all I needed to function optimally, and since I hadn't cared about taste, flavor had been unnecessary.

Pippa grabbed my hand and tugged me toward her food processor where the screen was lit up with a dozen pictures of different meal options. "I tried to narrow it down for you; there's like two hundred different meal options daily. You can work your way up to the full menu."

It was a small act of care, something another man might have overlooked as his due. It made me swallow hard. Decisions were hard to make for the soulless, especially ones with no clearly logical answer. So much of choice involved tiny emotional inputs that a person didn't notice until they were gone. And just because my emotions were back didn't mean the last seven years of habit was suddenly erased.

I squeezed my mate's hand and studied the menu. Even twelve options was overwhelming, and eventually I just chose the dish that my eye kept coming back to, a vegetable stir fry with some sort of brown sauce.

Pippa chose her own meal in a quarter of the time it took me, but she didn't make a comment about it, and in a couple of minutes, our meals were ready.

The vegetables on my plate were so colorful, orange and green and red. Colors seemed more vibrant now, and when I took a bite, the flavor exploded on my tongue. I devoured the food like a starving man, and when I looked up from my empty bowl, Pippa was less than halfway done with her meal.

Again, she didn't mention it.

It was a relief. Everything felt new and strange, and I needed to find a way to adjust without giving myself away. I felt like a different man, a new man, even if, perhaps, I was the same person I'd been before undergoing the soulless procedure.

Pippa tapped her utensil against her bowl, a nervous action. "I went to see the woman who was attacked earlier." She told me what she saw, and I tried not to imagine Pippa in that same place, unprotected and vulnerable.

My claws itched to shoot out, to stave off whatever threat there was to my mate.

"If she can identify her attacker, she may be in danger," I said. "Were there any guards? Station security?"

Pippa shook her head. "No, I walked right in. But the infirmary is still probably the safest place for her right now. I hope so, at least." She shuddered.

"The attacks are escalating." It went from Pippa, to Fran, to Pippa's attack, and now this woman. Whoever was doing this, their violence couldn't be assuaged.

"We need to stop it." Her voice was firm.

I couldn't disagree.

She finished her food and took both of our plates to her washer. Then she leaned back against the counter. "I was thinking about this whole mating bond thing today."

"Yes?" It thrummed brightly between us, almost a physical thing. If I closed my eyes, I thought I could see it.

"It's not ... That is ... you're not jealous, are you?" Her expression became worried, lips pursed and eyebrows drawn down.

"Jealous how?" It came out harsher than I meant, and I'd need to learn to control these kinds of reactions; I was seven years out of practice.

Pippa gave me a look. "Growling doesn't help

right now. It's just ... I saw Darian today, and I felt, I don't know, weird about it. He asked me to grab dinner with him, and I really didn't want to. And all that's new is this bond between us. Is it going to be like that every time one of my male friends wants to spend time with me? Because if so, not cool."

I didn't like Darian. I didn't want my denya spending time with him. But I didn't think it had anything to do with jealousy. I couldn't help but see him as a threat to the soulless Detyens on Nebula Outpost.

"The bond is between us," I told her. "It shouldn't effect how you react to others. And it's not my place to tell you which of your friends you can see."

Her expression grew serious, and she pushed off of the counter to take her seat beside me at the table. "Yeah, about telling me who I can and can't see ... apparently Ryklin doesn't think the same way you do."

"What?" Something dark and dangerous thundered through me.

"He told me to take Noelle and get off Nebula Outpost. He said you were a danger to us both. I didn't tell him about the bond between us, but I don't think it would have helped." She reached out and took my hand. "He offered me credits to leave. And ..." She pulled her hand back. "Drex, is there any way that Ryklin might be the killer?"

"No." My answer was immediate and harsh. "Absolutely not."

Pippa nodded, but she clearly wasn't convinced. "Hear me out, okay? He knows how to get into locked rooms. He knew about Sector X from his job. He might have had access to the jettison controls. And he's trying to get one of the people looking into the murder to leave. It's not nothing."

"I have the same access he does. By your logic, I could also be the killer. And so could you. Anyone in maintenance or groundskeeping could be. And Ryklin is soulless; he wouldn't murder out of passion."

"But he would murder?" she asked.

It was the harsh truth of our kind. "If it was necessary, then yes. And he'd feel no guilt. He can't." I didn't tell her what happened to the soulless, what he'd do to me if he found out about my relationship with Pippa. I'd find a way out of that; I just needed more time to think. "Let's go over what we know. We've been looking into this for days; if we lay it all out, maybe something will start to make sense."

We spent the rest of the night trying to follow

what clues we had to the evil stalking the ship, but every path we went down lead to a dead end. Pippa didn't bring up Ryklin again, but she had to be considering him.

We were missing something obvious, and I knew it. Did station security have the missing piece to this puzzle? Or was the attacker roaming free, cozy in the knowledge that they weren't going to get caught?

I made love to my mate with a fervor that night, and I held her close while we slept.

The longer this investigation went on, the more danger both of us were in. But in seven years, I'd lost the ability to hope, and I couldn't see how this ended with us anything other than battered and bloody.

And if we were lucky, it wouldn't end with us dead.

24

DREX

I DIDN'T WANT to leave my mate's side the next day. Her bed was warm. Her body was soft and smelled like home. If I were a rich man, I'd lay at her side forever with no care for what was going on outside.

But my communicator was buzzing with the reminder that I had a shift to get to, and Pippa had her own work to do. And all the while both of us had to be on the lookout for the killer stalking the station.

"We'll figure it out," she promised me with a lingering kiss once I was properly dressed and about to head out the door. "I trust you." There was something under those words that I couldn't decipher, something deeper.

I kissed her again, backing her up against the

wall and pressing my body against hers until all I could feel was her and the blood pumping hard in my veins. I could have taken her right there, but my comm buzzed again, and I pulled back.

"I'll see you tonight," I promised.

My shift dragged on. Some of the bushes in Sector H were looking a bit unhealthy, so I had to spend my shift digging around to look for any debris that could be causing it before seeding the soil with extra plant food and hoping it was enough. It was dirty, tedious work and left my mind completely free to wander.

Perhaps being soulless hadn't been all bad if it had allowed me to do this work without the crushing weight of boredom threatening to drive me to madness. I'd need to relearn how to deal with boredom. I must have once known how to do it.

But it couldn't be relearned in a day, and when my shift ended, I was glad of it.

I was on my way back to my quarters to retrieve a change of clothes when I realized it would have been wise to put my mind to work at analyzing everything I knew about the attacks on the station. But I couldn't go back in time to use it more wisely, so I'd have to consider that for tomorrow.

"Drex, wait," Ryklin called from behind me. My

claws pricked at my skin, every instinct screaming something was wrong.

Pippa thought Ryklin was the killer. Everything I knew about the warrior told me it wasn't true, but there was an inkling of doubt.

I was hiding my emotions from him, could he be hiding something dark and twisted from me?

I waited. I had to act like my old self around him, had to give him no reason to think something had changed within me.

He caught up, and his eyes flicked from my head to toe, taking in the smudges of dirt on my coveralls. "Come with me," he said, nodding his head towards the lifts and away from our quarters.

Those instincts were screaming even louder now. But there was nothing unusual here. The soulless didn't engage in useless questions. The Drex of last week would follow Ryklin without hesitation. I'd had no reason to distrust him.

I still had no reason to distrust him. Pippa didn't know him; she didn't know the soulless. Her evidence was completely circumstantial and could have applied to a hundred people on the ship, including me, and most of it also applied to her.

The fact that our suspect pool was only growing

was a sign that, perhaps, we weren't the best people to be running this investigation.

Ryklin pressed a button for the sixth level, and the lift moved.

"Does this have something to do with our investigation?" I finally asked. It was relevant. The soulless me might have made the same inquiry.

"Yes," Ryklin replied, but he didn't elaborate.

What would he say if I told him about Pippa's suspicions? I realized I didn't want to know what this Ryklin thought, but instead wanted to know what the Ryklin with a soul thought. What had he been like? We'd been in different units in the Legion, and though it was possible we'd met at some point, it hadn't been memorable. I'd only ever known the soulless version of this man.

Who had he been before he sacrificed everything?

At least he was still thinking about the case. Maybe he'd had more success at uncovering the villain than Pippa or me.

"Have you made any headway into discovering who jettisoned Sector X?" I asked.

"I have not," was all he said.

Then why were we here?

Level six was where our groundskeeping crew

kept most of our equipment and storage, though some of that storage was actually corralled in an area outside the station and retrieved via robotic arms that were attached to the exterior.

It was quiet now with the day shift being over.

Perhaps Ryklin just wanted a place to talk where we wouldn't be overheard.

He led me into the large storage hangar and finally stopped. "You spent another night with the human," he said.

"Yes." Some excuse sprang to my tongue, but I quashed it. I owed Ryklin no explanation, and the soulless me wouldn't think to offer one.

"You've fixated on her."

The accusation hit me like a punch to the gut, and I took a step back. "I have not." I'd worried that was what was happening, but now I knew otherwise. I'd only hoped I'd have more time to come up with a way to explain.

Ryklin clearly didn't believe me. "Your behavior has been erratic ever since you rescued that woman from the incinerator. At first, I believed it was merely a disruption to your normal routine that was causing the anomaly, but it has become clear over the last few days that is not the case. And for some reason, the woman refused to heed my warning."

"I'd never hurt Pippa." Even thinking about it wounded me to my core. I'd lay down my life for hers in a heartbeat. She was my heart; it wasn't even in question.

"All of the fixated believe that at first. And then it turns violent. We've seen the documentation. We know the warning signs. And we know what must be done." He reached into his pocket. "This will not hurt."

"I'm not fixated, she's my denya!" The confession tore out of me, and there was no mistaking the emotion in my voice.

It made Ryklin pause. "That's impossible."

"That's what I thought. Of course, I was worried that I'd fixated, but the bond is there. It's real. She's my mate, and my soul is reawakened. I feel, Ryklin. My emotions, all of it, it's there." I pounded my hand against my chest, letting all of my defenses drop in the hopes he might see me and understand.

Instead, he pulled a blaster out of his pocket. "You're further gone than I suspected if you're this delusional. What you say is impossible. Now stand beside the airlock; you know what I must do."

It was standard procedure. Once a soulless warrior fixated on something, there was no going back, and the only solution was death. We'd all understood this might happen to any one of us one day. But I was not fixated, and I wouldn't let Ryklin murder me.

"I'm not fixated, Ryklin," I said it again, hoping the impossible hope that he'd believe me. But there was no way to prove it. "She's my mate."

He leveled the blaster at me. "Then know you're protecting her."

Bullshit.

Ryklin fired the blaster, but I dove out of the way before the stun ray could hit me. Blasters weren't meant to be lethal, but they could be modified to deliver a killing blow. Ryklin didn't want to just knock me out, and he'd brought me here so he could easily dump my body outside.

No one would know where I'd gone.

Pippa.

No matter what, I couldn't leave Pippa.

The storage room offered many places to hide, but none of them would cover me for long. The entrance was several meters away, and if I went straight for it, Ryklin would find me. Even worse, it wouldn't take him long to realize there was only one realistic entrance.

I didn't want to take another space walk.

The moment he realized his advantage, he'd

plant himself at the door and wait me out. All I had to do was make one mistake and I was a dead man.

I'd sacrificed my soul for the Legion. I'd lived as a waking ghost for seven years. I wasn't going to lose this second chance at life because my comrade didn't understand what was happening to me and refused to believe a miracle when it was right in front of his face.

I didn't want to hurt Ryklin. Even as fear made me sweat and worry nipped at the back of my mind, I couldn't hold this against him. He was doing what he thought was right, trying to protect the rest of the soulless on the ship and Pippa.

I could yell out again, try and plead my case and hope something made him believe me. But all that would do was give away my position, and he'd be on me in seconds.

Footsteps echoed strangely in this huge storage room, but they were coming closer. He knew he had the upper hand. He was armed; he'd planned this out. But I was a cornered man, and there was nothing more dangerous than that.

I was crouched behind a forklift that still had a payload in front of it. Metal bars for some construction project.

Perfect.

I reached in and grabbed one, the metal warming in my hand. It was thinner than I would have liked and heavier than I expected, but it would do the job if Ryklin got anywhere near me.

My claws threatened to shoot out, but I kept them sheathed. If I played this right, Ryklin would survive it. If my claws came out, I'd tear him to shreds.

Anger. So that was what was simmering under the disappointment and fear. Ah, an old friend I'd forgotten. Yes, I was angry enough to spit, but I couldn't let it control me.

Footsteps again, closer this time. He was making his way through the narrow aisles, trying to find me and end this quickly.

The shadows were dark and deep in here; Ryklin hadn't turned on the overhead lights when we arrived. What little lighting we had was the auxiliary system that was triggered by any movement. Enough to navigate by, but not much more.

I nestled as deep into one of the shadows as I could and slowed my breathing to almost nothing. If he saw me first, I was dead. But he was getting closer every second and moving would only draw his attention.

There.

I heard him walking, breathing, getting closer and closer. I had to get that blaster out of his hand. Once he was disarmed, the playing field was level.

He turned down the aisle where I hid, and I prayed to any god that was listening that he didn't see me.

He walked right past me.

I stepped out of the shadow and swung the bar I was holding with all my might. Ryklin went down, the blaster clattering to the floor beside him. He groaned in pain, but I hopped over his prone body before he could reach his weapon again. I kicked it out of the way, and it slid under the forklift.

I couldn't get to it without getting on all fours and reaching, and I wasn't going to take the risk.

For half a second, I considered hitting Ryklin with the bar again, but instead I threw it aside and kicked him in the ribs. He reached for my leg, but he was too dazed to catch it before I could pull away.

I sprinted for the door.

Ryklin would be back up in no time. I had to get to Pippa before he found me again.

25
PIPPA

Hey, girl, there's an insane meteor shower happening off of Viewing Deck Three, come check it out.

The message from Noelle was sitting on my comm. I hadn't heard from Drex all day, but that wasn't too weird.

He was coming to see me later, all was well. Or as well as it could be with a killer on the loose.

I was tempted to tell Noelle no. But she was my best friend, and we'd barely seen each other in the last couple of weeks. I needed to spend time with her. I *wanted* to spend time with her. Besides, I could tell Drex to join us later. What kind of new emotions might a meteor shower unlock? When I thought of space too much, I ended up feeling very small and insignificant, but that wasn't the only way people felt. I wanted to give this to Drex, to let him uncover another piece of himself.

Mind made up, I headed for the door, but before I could leave, someone pounded on the door. I checked the viewer. It was Drex, with an intense worry on his face I'd never seen before.

I opened the door and ushered him in. "What's wrong? Has there been another death?"

He closed the door behind him and made sure it was locked. "We have to leave Nebula Outpost right now." His eyes darted around the room, looking for threats that weren't there.

"What? Drex? What's going on?" Everything had been fine this morning, but now he looked about a second away from slinging me over his shoulder and dragging me to the shuttle depot.

He found a satchel in my closet and stuffed it with a few changes of clothing. Then he reached for the picture of my parents I had hanging on my wall and added that. "He's going to come here. We have to get out before he does."

"Who? What? Take a second and explain. The killer?" His worry was making me worried, and I felt jittery from not understanding a thing.

Drex shoved the satchel at me, and I automatically slung it over my shoulder. "Ryklin. He just tried to kill me."

I knew it!

The triumph at solving this thing must have shown on my face because my mate shook his head. "It has nothing to do with the attacks. Ryklin thinks—Please, we need to leave now. I'll explain on the way."

I was frozen in place. Nebula Outpost was my home. The farthest I'd ever been from it was the surface of Nebula, and I could barely remember that. I'd been a little girl. I'd never really thought of leaving. And now Drex was trying to get me to take off in the middle of a murder investigation. If we left right now, there might never be justice for Fran.

If we stayed, Drex's life was in danger.

My fingers tightened on the strap of my satchel. "This better be a good explanation."

He let out a relieved breath. "Come on."

We were out the door and down the hall before I remembered Noelle's message. "We have to stop by Viewing Deck Three. It's right by the departure depot, and Noelle's there. I need to say goodbye." I couldn't believe this was happening, that I was really going along with this madness.

Drex's jaw tightened, and he looked back over

his shoulder, but we were alone in the hallway. "Only a goodbye," he relented. "There's no time to talk, to explain it to her."

I didn't like that. I didn't understand this at all. And he was walking so fast I had to jog-step to keep up. "Why did Ryklin try to kill you?" And how many killers was this station harboring? Everywhere we turned, it seemed like there was more violence.

Though my breaths were laboring, Drex didn't seem at all bothered by our pace. "He thinks I've fixated on you, that I'm a threat to you."

"Fixated?"

"It's something that happens to the soulless. We ... They become obsessed with a person to the exclusion of everything else. They can become violent, especially if someone tries to separate them. And they can hurt the person they've fixated on. We were all warned about it before we agreed to become soulless. Everyone knows it's possible. And there's only one thing to be done when it happens." He'd fallen back into that emotionless cadence of his. Voice flat and cold.

My mind automatically went to those first days with Drex, the intensity of his stare and the way he seemed drawn to me even if he couldn't feel a thing.

Knowing how it turned out, I couldn't see any bad in it, but from the outside ...

"Maybe if I talk to him it will help." I didn't want to run away, to leave everything I knew behind with so many loose ends hanging. And I didn't want Drex to leave his home either. This place was ours.

"I tried talking; it didn't work." Drex picked up his pace, and I was fully jogging now, breaths coming in fast and hard.

"But if he sees us together—"

He cut me off, voice harsh. "He can't understand it. He'll strike me down right in front of you as if it means nothing, and if he says a word to you, he'll tell you that you're now safe from me. He's soulless, Pippa. He can't understand this." Some of the emotion bled into his voice. The pain and heartache were enough to make me wince.

We had to leave now. I could see the conviction in Drex. But maybe it didn't have to be forever. We could take a vacation to some nearby planet, maybe one that had a beach, and give Ryklin time to cool off—or whatever the soulless equivalent of cooling off was. Then we could show him all was well, that Drex would never hurt me.

I had to believe that, had to believe we might be able to come home one day.

I almost told him to skip the goodbye to Noelle. I could message her from our transport. But she wouldn't forgive me if I took off like that, and there was still no sign of Ryklin. I could steal two minutes to say goodbye.

The hallway outside Viewing Deck Three was strangely empty considering meteor showers were pretty popular sights. Usually, they were announced ahead of time, and people threw parties to celebrate. But sometimes the smaller ones passed by unnoticed.

Drex gave a final look down the hallway. "Make this quick," he warned.

"I will." I thought he'd stand guard in the hall-way, but he walked right beside me through the door.

The room was dark, and I couldn't see anyone waiting. Had I read the message wrong? I was about to pull out my comm to check when Drex's fingers curled tight around my wrist.

Then there was a flash of light, and Drex grunted and crashed to the floor.

26

PIPPA

I SCREAMED. Everything went fuzzy in my head, and I knelt over my mate, the sudden surety that he was dead crashing over me in a crushing wave. But he was still groaning in pain, writhing on the floor.

And the side of his shirt was singed and smoking, a sure sign of a blaster shot.

"Pippa, run!" Noelle's voice cut off on a yelp of pain.

I was crouched behind the final row of seating in the viewing room. It meant I couldn't see where Noelle or Drex's attacker was, but it also meant we couldn't easily be shot again.

I didn't know what to do. I was completely frozen, hovering over my mate like touching him would heal a stun wound, and terrified that the attacker could find us any moment.

Trap.

And we'd walked right into it.

Again.

But a distant part of me realized that my attacker, Fran's killer, the monster stalking the ship, was in this room with us. And we were going to end this.

Now.

In a perfect world, Drex and I wouldn't have been in the middle of a run for our lives. He certainly wouldn't be shot, and he'd be armed with a weapon that I knew how to use. But that wasn't the world we were in now.

I could hear footsteps slowly coming up the stairs, something dragging behind them as Noelle struggled.

I tugged on Drex, and he struggled to a sitting position. His blue face was covered in sweat, and his eyes looked dull with pain. "Come on, babe, we need to move." I kept my voice low, but it was so quiet in the room that the attacker could no doubt hear me.

"Poor little Pippa, what are we going to do about you?" The voice sent a chill down my spine.

I knew that voice.

I'd heard it nearly every day.

I'd thought it belonged to my friend.

Darian.

Rage fired through me, and if I had a blaster I'd stand right up and shoot him. Instead, I bit my tongue and poured all that passion into getting Drex to move. We were lucky Darian wasn't using a modified blaster, otherwise Drex would be dead.

But Darian wanted an audience for his cruelty. Even a mid-strength stun would have knocked my mate out, the fact that he was moving right now meant the stunner was on its lowest setting.

Drex was slow as we crouch walked backwards, trying to make it towards the door. But before we could make it, Darian stepped into that final row, holding Noelle in front of him like a human shield. He leveled the blaster right for us, and Drex dove down the stairway right in front of us, taking me with him.

My teeth clattered together as we tumbled down three steps before catching our balance.

"What are you doing, Darian?" I had a feeling running wasn't going to do much good. But maybe he wanted to talk. And any time I could buy us for Drex to recover was worth it. "Has this all been you?"

Darian barked out a harsh laugh, and Noelle whimpered. If he'd hurt her, I was going to pay back that pain a hundredfold. "I thought you were the smart one," he spat. "Pippa the genius, too good for the rest of us."

"What?" I didn't think a genius could feel as confused as I did.

"He's crazy!" Noelle yelled it before her voice was muffled again.

"All of you, thinking you're smarter than me. Better. All you had to do was wait, and it would all make sense. Let the bond snap into place and be done with it. It didn't have to happen this way." His voice was getting closer.

Drex was still in bad shape. I didn't want to think about what might happen if he got shot again.

"What bond, Darian?" I asked, but I had a sinking sensation I knew what he meant.

Detyens died young without their mates. Darian was trying to find his denya.

And killing anyone who didn't match.

"They think it's fate." His voice was intense. "It's never been fate. Fate doesn't exist. You just need the right conditions. We knew that on Detya, but everyone's forgotten."

Drex shook his head, though I wasn't sure it was to contradict Darian or to tell me something else.

"What conditions?" Stall. I needed to stall.

I could faintly make out light from the hallway behind Darian. The door hadn't fully shut when Drex and I walked in, and he was too in his own world to care.

"It's a biological imperative," he explained. "All you've gotta do is make her believe she needs you to survive. Then boom, bond!" The words were punctuated by a pained moan from Noelle.

I winced. He was hurting my friend, and there was nothing I could do to stop it. "How was locking me in that incinerator supposed to do that?" I could still feel the heat licking at my feet, and a tiny part of me would always be locked in that metal coffin.

"I was supposed to be the one to rescue you!" He got louder then, practically shouting it. "Not that broken excuse for a Detyen no one's ever seen before."

He stopped in front of the door.

I had to keep him talking.

"And what about Fran? You didn't save her." Had she pounded on the door like I had? Had she screamed?

"All she had to do was accept the bond!" His

voice was tinged with panicked anger. "She didn't need to die."

How long would he talk? All he had to do was come down the stairs, and we'd be at his mercy. He had the stunner, and I was no fighter.

But his options were limited as long as he kept his hold on Noelle. He had to keep an arm around her, and every time she struggled, it would mess with his aim. When would he decide she was more trouble than she was worth?

Even a low-level blaster shot right to the head might kill her.

"Why humans?" I'd noticed all the victims were human women, made a note of it somewhere. Maybe I should have paid more attention. Nebula Outpost was full of aliens from all over the galaxy.

"Everyone knows Detyens can mate with humans; haven't you heard about Earth? There aren't exactly any Detyen women on the ship. I wasn't taking any chances. So come on up here, Pip, and accept the bond. This can all end now."

I hadn't heard about Earth, and I had no idea what it had to do with his people, but I wasn't about to ask him anything.

He was crazy. Absolutely, violently, crazy. But I

wasn't stupid enough to say a word about my bond with Drex.

Darian would kill us all if he knew.

"Let go of Noelle first," I called. "Then I'll come." There was a flicker of shadow in the light of the doorway.

"Not a chance," Darian sneered. "Get your ass up here."

"You have your blaster on the hostage that you're holding right in front of you," I said it loudly and ignored Drex's puzzled look. "You can't expect me to walk right up those stairs when you can shoot my friend. Let her go. I'll take her place."

Drex reached out and clamped a hand on my ankle. I shook my head at him and gave him a wide-eyed look, hoping he would trust me.

"Come up here, and I'll let her go," Darian bargained.

Before I could even think about moving, the door behind him slid fully open, and Ryklin barreled into the room.

27
DREX

I HEARD THE COMMOTION, but my body still wouldn't cooperate. Every muscle was pressed down by a phantom weight with sensation slowly—and painfully—returning. Then there was a feminine scream, and it was enough to make adrenaline shoot through my veins and overpower the waning effects of the blaster shot.

There had always been something off about Darian, but I hadn't wanted to suspect another Detyen.

Pippa crouched down and gave me a panicked smile as her eyes roved over my injuries. "Ryklin just tackled Darian," she whispered quickly. "Noelle broke out of Darian's grasp. Can you move?"

I nodded. I had to.

I'd never been happier to have a fellow warrior hunting me. Ryklin was capable of prioritizing threats, and he'd save Pippa and Noelle before he tried to kill me.

I hoped.

Getting to my feet was a struggle, but I managed, and each step was easier than the last. We waddle stepped down the aisle to the far end and crept up the stairs. Noelle was curled against the wall, chest heaving as she sobbed.

Pippa rushed toward her and got an arm around her. I heard her urging the other woman on but couldn't make out exactly what she was saying.

We needed an exit.

Ryklin and Darian struggled in front of the door and had barely moved. Though Ryklin was a trained warrior, Darian refused to give an inch.

Pippa and Noelle needed to get out of here.

As long as they were in this room, Darian could use them. All he had to do was get close enough to shoot them. If he hurt Pippa ...

I gave my mate a look, and her eyes widened.

"Whatever you're thinking, don't," she said, shaking her head. "You're hurt."

I flexed my hand, and my claws shot out. "When the path is clear, take her, get out, and summon station security." They'd been completely useless so far, but maybe now, when we could hand them the killer on a silver platter, they'd help.

Her jaw firmed, and she narrowed her eyes, but then she looked beyond me to where Ryklin and Darian fought. She gave a tight nod. "If you die, I'll never forgive you."

I leaned close and gave her a quick kiss, pouring whatever passion I could into three seconds before I forced myself to back off.

Then I was on my feet and sprinting for the fighting Detyens. Darian didn't see me coming. My claws raked down his back, and he screamed.

Ryklin took the opportunity to get a good punch in, but Darian must have had some training. He rolled to the side and retreated down the center aisle of the viewing room, Ryklin hot on his heels.

Good.

I was right there with them, but with the element of surprise gone, the hits didn't come so easy. Perhaps if Ryklin and I had experience as a fighting unit it might have made a difference, but we'd cornered a desperate man, and there was no one more dangerous.

The entryway at the top of the steps briefly brightened as Pippa and Noelle made their escape.

"No!" Darian tried to charge, and Ryklin punched again.

He kept trying to get past us. His eyes were wild, and he kept calling out to them, as if one of the women would actually turn around and come back.

He really was crazy.

And with his focus on the women, he barely noticed me creeping behind him. I wrapped my arm around his neck and got him in a choke tight enough to control him. If I tightened my arm the tiniest bit, it would be over.

If I held on for more than a few seconds, he'd be dead.

"It's over, Darian," I said. Over his shoulder, I met Ryklin's eyes.

I don't know what I expected to see, some acknowledgement of the help I'd given him, some sign that he understood that I wasn't fixated on Pippa. Something that told me that this would be alright.

"Keep him there," Ryklin instructed while heading back up the steps.

I wrapped my other arm around one of Darian's arms to keep him from trying anything. But Darian didn't struggle. It was as if the fight had gone out of him when he was caught, and now he was waiting for the end.

I turned us both to watch Ryklin's movements, but it was too dark to make out much in the viewing room.

"I—" Darian tried to speak.

I tightened my grip. He'd said enough already. There was a flash of light, and Darian's body went completely limp. I struggled to hold him up for just a second as realization dawned.

The damned blaster. Ryklin had Darian's weapon.

I dropped Darian's limp form and dove right back into the same aisle Pippa and I had sought cover in. "I'm not fixated on Pippa!" I yelled. I wasn't giving away my position. Ryklin knew exactly where I was, and this time, he wasn't going to make the same mistake he had in the storage room.

There was one door out of this theater, and he would wait there until the end of time.

But Pippa was coming back with station security. I only had to last that long.

"This is an honorable death," Ryklin said. There was none of Darian's manic desperation. "Set an example for our brethren. We always knew this would happen."

"It doesn't have to." When my commanding officer had put me on the transport to escape my execution, I hadn't understood it. I'd deviated. I'd malfunctioned. There was only one remedy to that. But now, I was beginning to understand why he'd gone against orders, why all of our commanding officers or colleagues had risked their positions, and in some cases their lives, to help us escape death sentences.

The soulless weren't machines who could be relied on to run their programming and nothing else. We—*they*—were still people with all the flaws that went along with that. And we didn't deserve to die because someone didn't understand why we made a decision.

"She's my mate, Ryklin. My denya. Maybe that's what fixation is, or could be, if we let it run its course. If I was fixated, I'd never have let her run with Noelle. I never would have stayed to fight." He was a being of logic; there had to be something I could say to get through to him.

But before he could respond, the door crashed open once more with half a dozen station security guards screaming for us to put our weapons down. A second later, there was a flash of light and a thump as someone blasted Ryklin.

He wouldn't be dead, I had to assure myself, angry on his behalf even if he'd been on the verge of killing me. He wasn't the bad guy here.

"I'm unarmed!" I yelled from my position. I didn't want to startle these security guards whose response to station bar fights was to blast everyone and let them wake up in the infirmary. I raised my hands—claws retracted—over my head and slowly stood.

The guards took one look at me and opened fire.

28

PIPPA

"You bring your supervisor down here right now, or no one in station security will have properly calibrated temperature control in their quarters ever again!" I yelled it into the comm, my lip curled. My hand would have been shaking if I wasn't holding to comm so tight. My other hand was curled into a fist.

"Ma'am, that's not—" the operator struggled to reply.

"Now!" I ended the call with a glare. "Those bastards!" My heartbeat hadn't calmed down since the moment that unit from station security showed up and decided to treat everyone in the theater like a criminal. The unit leader had assured me that the blasters only knocked people out, that there'd never been an instance of this model killing someone.

As if knocking my mate out was justified.

The commander's ear still had to be ringing from how loud I'd yelled. I wish I could have done more. If I had claws like Drex's, I'd have done some real damage.

Noelle had been whisked off to the main station infirmary while Drex, Ryklin, and Darian were all in the smaller infirmary room manned by station security. It was where they observed the rowdiest of bar goers who they blasted on a weekly basis.

I'd been assured that once they woke up, this would all be sorted out. They knew Darian had abducted Noelle, and that was crime enough for him to face punishment. I'd told them he'd confessed to the rest of it, to some extent, and I only hoped he told them exactly what he'd done.

But Darian's threat was the least of my concerns now.

I'd been speaking to security for hours, and they'd finally left me alone, probably to escape my ever increasing wrath. I doubted the supervisor would show himself for at least an hour, if ever.

Somehow, I was going to make good on my threat.

But there was something I had to do first.

No one said a word as I walked down the short

hall from the interrogation room to the infirmary ward. I spotted my mate lying on one of the narrow cots, and my heart twisted with the need to go to him.

But I stepped right by. Not yet. He was still sleeping, but his fellow soulless Detyen had started to move as he shook off the effects of the blaster. Drex, having been shot twice tonight, would no doubt take longer to recover.

I sat on the edge of the cot, and Ryklin opened his eyes. He stared at me, completely awake. His hands were cuffed to the bed.

"You're in the infirmary in the station security wing," I told him. I spoke quietly enough so that I wouldn't be overheard. "And it's time you and I came to an understanding."

His eyes narrowed slightly, but he didn't speak.

"They haven't put together that you were hunting Drex," I told him. I could murder him right now for what he'd tried. But I'd forced myself to consider what my mate would want, what he'd said about Ryklin. And what all of the soulless had been through. "But one word from me and you're in a cell right next to Darian, and you'll be sent to a penal colony on the next shipment."

Ryklin remained silent.

"Drex told me about what you are. And he told me about fixation. He's my mate. He has emotions. I get that you don't understand it, that it's new, but I'm not going to let you kill him for it." I stood up from the bed before I punctuated my statement with a swift poke to one of his wounds. Darian had managed a few nasty blows before he went down. "Are we clear?"

Ryklin's tongue darted out to lick his lips. "Water." It was a rasping word.

I grabbed the small cup on the bedside table and held the straw to his mouth so he could take a sip.

This time when he spoke, it wasn't so raspy. "What you're saying is impossible."

"So are you." Detyens couldn't live past thirty; that was the curse of their species. But Ryklin and the other soulless were living proof that was a lie. There was a heavy cost, a cost so many would be unwilling to pay if given the chance, but the possibility existed. "What's it going to be, Ryklin?"

He was quiet for a long moment, thinking it over. "He lives," he conceded.

"Glad we understand each other." I stood.

"More water?" he asked.

"I'm not your nurse." I left his bed and went to sit by my mate. And though more than two hours passed, he didn't wake up.

29
NOELLE

I COULDN'T STOP JUMPING at shadows.

"You're fine," I told myself as I had to walk down the hallway where Darian had ambushed me. There was a dark alcove that I'd never paid any attention to before. That was where he'd waited, how he'd grabbed me.

For the past three days, ever since I'd gotten out of the infirmary, I'd been going the long way back to my quarters to avoid it. Every step added onto the walk made me feel like a coward.

Nebula Outpost had been my home for six years. I'd arrived on this distant station and felt a sense of rightness that I'd never felt back in The Consortium. I'd known from the first night that this was where I was meant to be.

And now, that feeling was gone.

Every time I closed my eyes, I saw Darian's face as he ranted about the women he'd killed. He'd stared deep into my eyes and told me that all I had to do was accept him, and he'd be the one. Whatever that was supposed to mean.

Thank the gods he wasn't.

If he'd been my mate, I would have jumped out the airlock rather than submit. He was a monster. And he'd be punished.

But that did nothing to soothe my nightmares.

I quickstepped down the hallway, past the alcove, and made the final turn to my own hallway. Maybe I could check in on Pippa and her man. It was taking him some time to shrug off the effects of blaster fire, and maybe she could use another pair of hands.

I didn't want to be alone.

And despite my hyper-vigilance, I didn't see the hulking blue form turning down the hall until I bumped into him.

Darian.

No. Darian was in a cell awaiting transport to a prison colony, never to be free again.

Ryklin.

They didn't really look alike, but that moment of

false recognition had sent my heartbeat into over-drive. And from what Pippa had told me about this Detyen, I didn't like him much more than Darian.

Not that she'd told me much. There was something strange going on with Drex and his companions, but Pippa kept her mouth shut, and I hadn't pushed.

We all had our secrets.

We stood there frozen for several seconds. I wasn't sure what to say. Words had never failed me before, but ever since that night, I found my tongue all tied up, and I couldn't untangle the knot.

"You seem recovered," Ryklin finally said.

"Physically, yes." I gave him a tight smile.

We lapsed back into silence. I was only a few meters from the privacy of my own quarters, but now it felt like a light year. But years of training were too ingrained in me to snub the man who'd rescued me. Or, at least half rescued me.

"Darian was transported yesterday evening. He will not trouble you again." Ryklin's voice was steady, monotone, really. Maybe he was dealing with his own mental crap too.

"You'd think there'd be a trial or something." My former home on Thanatos hadn't exactly been a bastion of democracy and freedom, but accused criminals still had to go before a judge; they still got to make their defense.

"His crimes will be reviewed by the judicial board of the Nebula System Penal Colony."

As far as I was concerned, they could throw him in a deep pit and forget about him forever. "Did you come up here to let Drex know that? You're his friend, right?" Always keep the conversation going. Ask questions. Smile. Amazing how all of that was still there even when my stomach was about three seconds away from hurling up its contents due to thoughts of Darian.

Ryklin tilted his head down and looked away. His expression remained neutral. "I'm ... I don't think Drex would like to see me right now."

"Oh." Never get too close. Don't pry at clear wounds unless you're trying to hurt. Only hurt people on purpose.

Mother would be so proud of me if she heard me repeating her poison.

"I need to ..." I nodded towards my room and took a step back, half-fearing that Ryklin would grab for me. It's what happened the last time I'd stopped in the hallway to chat with someone.

"Of course. Goodbye." He continued walking down the hallway.

Once I was in my quarters, I let out a heavy breath and leaned back against the door. Would Nebula Outpost ever feel like home again?

———

RYKLIN

The door to Noelle's apartment closed behind her. I settled into the small alcove and observed it.

She lived only two doors down from Pippa. And now Drex, I assumed.

Zyrus had collected Drex's belongings into a small bag yesterday, but he hadn't told me where he was taking them. I hadn't asked. I had no right to ask.

Had I done the wrong thing?

Before I lost my soul, I might have called doubt an emotion. But now I knew it was a toxic sludge that ate away at every decision no matter how logical it was.

How could I know Drex had found his denya? I'd never heard of a soulless Detyen finding a mate, let alone any Detyen mating with a human. Impossibility piled on top of impossibility. We soulless were logical creatures above anything else; there was no reason to suspect the impossible.

I didn't know why I was lurking in this hallway. It must have been that I wanted to understand this change in Drex. We'd lived alongside each other for years, as close to friends—some might even say brothers—as two could be.

And at the first sign of deviation from the expected, I'd tried to put him down.

There was no guilt. I couldn't feel that.

Just doubt.

And something else nipping at the back of my mind. If I was up here to observe Drex, why was I in this alcove? I couldn't see his door. I was cut off from the rest of the hallway.

But I could see Noelle's.

I'd been aware of the human in a peripheral sort of way ever since she'd come to repair some of the lighting on one of the landscapes I'd worked on months ago. I'd see her from time to time, and something in the back of my brain always noticed.

Not fixation. Just ... observation.

No need to think too much about it, to let the doubts creep in.

I stayed in the alcove for a long time, waiting for answers that never came.

30
PIPPA

"Here we go, just like grandma used to make. Probably." I gently placed the soup bowl in front of Drex and handed him a spoon.

"I'm fully recovered," he assured me. "No need to treat me like an invalid."

There were dark circles under his eyes, and his blue skin looked a little green in places, some from bruising, some from the sallowness that came from lying in an infirmary bed for a day and a half.

"It's soup, not a med scanner." I nudged the bowl his way. "Healthy people can eat soup." It was full of ginger and vegetables, and everything that made you healthy. And it smelled good enough that I had a bowl waiting for me on the counter. I got up and grabbed it, just to emphasize my point.

With my own bowl in front of me, my mate began to eat.

Good.

His color didn't immediately improve, but I let myself believe him when he said he was fine. Two shots from a blaster and a three-way fight between Detyens—two of them trained warriors—would take a bit of time for anyone to recover from.

"Darian's gone," I told him. "The supervisor from station security told me himself." There'd been no thanks when I'd offered what evidence Drex and I had managed to collect. In the end, it wasn't really that much. I wasn't sure we would have ever come around to Darian if he hadn't tried to kill us all.

Or force a mating bond.

How did he even think that would work?

"Dead?" Drex asked. He said it so casually that I had to pause for a moment to make sure I'd heard him right.

"Transported to a penal colony. Nebula's an out of the way system, and we're in this even more out of the way pocket of it, but we're not the only settle-ment. I guess everyone sends the hard cases there." I'd heard stories of the penal colony before, but it was always something to scare children. I'd never heard of anyone actually being sent there.

I hoped I never heard of it again.

Drex just nodded and finished his soup.

"Did you hear what he said about humans and Detyens? What was that about Earth?" I'd thought that everything Darian had ranted about should be pushed to the back of my mind and ignored forever. But clearly Detyens *could* mate with humans. I was living proof of that.

"I don't know," said Drex. "Perhaps some Detyens have settled on Earth? I'm sure if it's something big we can look into it." He didn't seem too concerned.

I made a mental note to hit up the data banks later and see if there was news. Maybe Darian was blowing something out of proportion. Or maybe Drex would like an update on his people. I knew I would.

His things were nestled into one drawer in my closet. His colleague, Zyrus, had brought an unbelievably small bag containing three sets of clothes, two pairs of shoes, and some underwear.

That was all Drex had.

Whenever I looked at those things, a pang went through me. Five years on this station, and all he had was half a drawer's worth of clothing. Nothing personal. Nothing to remember his home by.

I knew he'd been soulless, that he couldn't have cared about that stuff if he wanted to, but it made me sad. And I couldn't help but imagining five other small sets of clothes in the cramped quarters down on level seven.

Drex had warned me not to think about it. Yes, he'd found me, and our bond had given him his emotions back. But there was no reason to think it would happen a second time.

The softer feelings for his brethren didn't extend to Ryklin. I hoped his shoes got holes in them and his socks were always damp. He'd tried to kill my mate for the crime of loving me. I'd never forgive that.

"Are you going to tell the others what's going on with you?" I asked. Zyrus hadn't lingered to chat, but he must have seen enough to notice there was only one bed in these quarters.

"There's a risk," he said. His voice was edging back into that soulless, monotonous tone. He did that sometimes, and it made my guts curdle, a distant fear that he might lose his emotions again, that he might be sitting right here but there would be an iron wall of nothingness between us. "Fixation is real; I've seen it. Shortly before I became soulless, there was a soulless warrior in my unit who fixated on a local woman. He nearly murdered her husband, kidnapped her, and barricaded himself in a small house. She managed to escape. By then he was cornered. He blew up the house rather than be captured."

Darian wasn't soulless, but the story reminded me of him nonetheless. Violence. Desperation. At least part of that was written into the Detyen DNA.

"I don't think telling them you found your mate will make them more likely to fixate on someone. They've been here for years without that happening. And you're still going to see them around, right? They'll figure something's up eventually." The soulless might not have emotions, but nothing suggested they were stupid.

"I'll figure out something to say." But he didn't look happy about it.

At least he looked like he was feeling something. Not many women would celebrate their lover's frowns, but I'd embrace every part of Drex, so long as I knew that he was feeling. I never wanted that to stop.

"What if it happened again?" I couldn't help but asking. "What if one of them finds their denya?"

His face softened, hope beginning to bloom. But he schooled his expression just as quickly. "There's no reason to think it could."

"Because we're so special?" I was a maintenance engineer; he was a landscaper. We weren't exactly the kinds of people destiny chose for anything.

"You are special," he said as he reached out and pulled me out of my chair until I was straddling his lap.

His eyes flared red as he pulled me down to kiss me. I opened my mouth, surrendering fully to the sensation.

This felt like destiny. Right here in his arms.

His fingers wound through my hair and tugged, angling me for better access, and I moaned.

I needed more. I always would.

I was still discovering everything he liked, the little sensitive spots that made him growl and hold me tighter. I felt like I'd known him forever, but this thing between us was still so new.

But not fragile.

Never that.

I tilted my head to the side, and Drex teased my neck, nipping lightly in the same spot he'd marked me that first night we came together, that claiming we hadn't realized would bind us together forever. "I love you," I whispered. The words fell easily, already so natural on my tongue.

I'd said it over and over again while he lay unconscious in the infirmary, and he'd woken up to those words on my lips. I didn't think I'd ever stop saying it.

He ran his hand down my thigh and cupped my ass, holding me closer against him. "Love you," he said against my neck, the words vibrating against my skin until I shivered.

Perfect.

He tugged the hem of my shirt until I lifted my arms, and he swept it over my head, leaving me bare from the waist up. Drex's eyes flared red again, and he leaned down to press a kiss to the upper slope of my breast. He took my nipple into his mouth and flicked it with his tongue, rolling the bud with his teeth.

My hips bucked against him, and I squirmed on his lap, desperate for something more. Drex growled, and I could feel his hard length in his pants.

I wanted it inside me.

But Drex wanted to play, and I was at his mercy.

His hand on my butt squeezed and guided my hips into a slow grinding circle that made me feel every inch of him. He licked and nipped at my breast, playing with one before he switched to the other.

Desperate to touch him, I tugged at his shirt, pulling it over his head until he, too, was giving me some skin. Then my hands were on him, skimming his pecs and abs, tracing the lines of those dark marks that covered his gorgeous blue skin. I scraped my nails down his chest, and he groaned.

"I want you." My voice was feral, so full of need I barely recognized it.

In a burst of movement, Drex surged up, taking me with him. He swiped aside our dinner bowls, clearing enough space on the table to lay me out.

I was his feast.

"Do you love these pants?" he asked, a ferocious gleam in his eye.

I had a feeling I knew where this was going and couldn't stop my grin. "Not at all."

His claws flashed out and raked down my hips, tearing through fabric without doing any damage to my skin. It took an insane amount of control, and I wouldn't have trusted anyone else to do it.

But this was my mate. I trusted him with everything.

Drex breathed deep as he looked down at me, laid out before him like a pagan sacrifice. His eyes flared red as he freed himself from his own pants. His claws were gone now as he cradled his cock in one hand, giving it a lazy stroke.

I bit my lip and stared. Stars above, he was gorgeous. And all mine.

He leaned down and kissed me, pressing our foreheads together for just a heartbeat. I couldn't see what he was doing, but I gasped when I felt his cock press against my entrance, the thick head teasing me, promising everything.

"Ready?" he asked me.

Was that really a question? "Always."

With one smooth thrust, he filled me, my body clenching tight around him as I moaned. One of Drex's hands came up and tweaked my nipple, twisting the pleasure until I was begging him to move.

Slowly, too slowly, he pulled almost all the way out before filling me once again. It was torture, divine, exquisite torture that made me beg for more.

I gripped the edge of the table and held on as Drex gave me all the stimulation I craved, fucking me deeply and steadily, his powerful body driving my need higher and higher. His lips found my ear, and as he bit at the soft lobe, "Come for me," he ordered, and I exploded. Pleasure washed over me, bright and beautiful.

Drex kept pounding me, drawing out my climax until I thought I would combust. He shuddered and came with a deep growl, filling me with his release.

I collapsed on the table. He loomed over me, eyes blazing. He leaned forward and pressed a soft kiss to my mouth, and somehow it was more intense than everything that had preceded it.

"I love you, denya," he whispered.

The syllables that came out of my mouth weren't words, but from the smile on his face, he knew exactly what I meant.

Thank you for reading Dangerous Bond!
I'd appreciate it so much if you would consider leaving a review.

The Detyen Warrior Outcast series continues with **Intrepid Bond.**

NEED A BIT MORE OF DANGEROUS BOND?

Sign up at the link below to **receive a free bonus story!** What happened when Drex first came to Nebula Outpost?

Find out now!
https://katerudolph.net/index.php/dangerous-bond-bonus/

———

Looking for EVEN MORE alien romance?

Detyens are doomed to die young if they don't find their fated mates.

Could humans be the answer to their prayers?

When Ruwen meets Lis, a human woman on the run from her nasty alien abductors their story changes the fate of a doomed alien race...

Journey into the world of **Mated to the Alien** where you'll find fierce women, protective heroes, fated mates, and a galaxy big enough to blow your mind!

Learn more

ALSO BY KATE RUDOLPH

Mated to the Alien

Fated Mate Alien Romance

Detyens are doomed to die young if they don't find their fated mates.

Follow along as these mated pairs fight off aliens, corrupt dictators, prejudiced humans, pirates, and more! The books can be read or listened to in any order, though some characters show up in multiple stories.

Select books available in audio.

Pick a book and jump into the action today!

Ruwen

Tyral

Stoan

Cyborg

Krayter

Kayleb

Shayn

Braxtyn

Doryan

Dekon

———

Detyen Warriors
Detya was destroyed a hundred years ago. These doomed warriors are out to find justice... and their mates.
The Detyen Warriors series brings you kick butt heroines, alpha alien heroes, fated mates, and relationships strong enough to span the galaxy!
The entire series is also available in audio!

Soulless

Ruthless

Heartless

Faultless

Endless

———

Guarded by the Shifter

Werewolf. Bodyguard. Mate.
The origins of these shifters are shrouded in mystery, but they're determined to protect their mates from any harm that comes their way.
Also available in audio!
Hunting Season
On the Prowl
Stalking Magic
Wolf Cursed
Hungry for the Wolf
Wolf's Temptation

———

Stealing the Alpha

The thief takes what she wants, but the alpha keeps what's his...
Join shifter thief Mel as she clashes with lion alpha Luke in an explosive trilogy of two opposites who can't keep away from one another.
Also available in audio!
The Alpha Heist

Entangled with the Thief
In the Alpha's Bed

Alien Mates: Planet Exile

Guerran is no place for pretty human women. But these alien heroes will protect their mates!
Also available in audio!

Exile's Hunter
Exile's Adored

Zulir Warrior Mates

Kidnapped humans. Alien Warriors. Electric wings.
The Zulir Warrior Mates series brings you human heroines and heroes abducted from Earth who find love – and wings! – with the alien warriors who rescue them.
Also available in audio!
Synnr's Saint

Synnr's Hope

Synnr's Spark

Synnr's Kiss

Synnr's Ride

Dragon Brides

Dragon Princes. Fierce Women. Love.

Fated mates, fierce women, and dragon princes are
ready to find their mates.

Crux

Ranger

Saber

Cipher

Storm

Drake

Asher

Knox

Flint

Alien Holiday Romance

Christmas... in space????
These alien holiday romances look beyond Earth's winter holidays and ring in the season across the galaxy!
Select titles available in audio.
Snowed in with the Alien Beast
The Alien's Winter Gift
The Alien Reindeer's Wild Ride
Trapped with her Alien Mate

––––––

Alien Outlaws

Outlaws, schemes, and love... it's all there in the Alien Outlaws series...
Andie Munster is sick of life on Ixilta, the planet she got dumped on after being abducted from Earth six years ago. And when the mysterious and dangerous Xandr shows up looking for a way off the planet, she's half-prisoner, half-co-conspirator in a wild rush to escape.
Rogue Alien's Escape
Rogue Alien's Woman
Rogue Alien's Secret
Rogue Alien's Legacy

———

Find more by Kate Rudolph at www.
katerudolph.net

ABOUT KATE RUDOLPH

Kate Rudolph is a paranormal and sci-fi romance writer who lives in Indiana. She loves writing about kick butt heroines and the steamy heroes who love them. She's been devouring romance novels since she was too young to be reading them and had to hide her books so no one would take them away. She couldn't imagine a better job in this world than writing romances and sharing them with her fellow readers.

If you enjoyed this story, please consider leaving a review.

www.ingramcontent.com/pod-product-compliance
Lightning Source LLC
Chambersburg PA
CBHW020756190726
48285CB00006B/2061